STUBBORN GIRL

FAÎTE FALLING
BOOK SEVEN

MARY E. TWOMEY

MARY E. TWOMEY

Stubborn Girl
Book Seven in the Faîte Falling Series

By

Mary E. Twomey

COPYRIGHT

DEDICATION

For April Nank,
whose patience and unfettered acceptance of everyone's quirks
makes me wish I was a better person.

On a side note,
one day I'll beg you to get me organized.
That day is not today.

A MOTHER AND HER DAUGHTER

If anyone ever thought to put together a manual about what to do if an immortal had a full-blown heart attack out of nowhere, I would read that book. Or, more accurately, I'd have someone else read it to me.

Kerdik grasped his chest as I held him on the floor of my bedroom, panting in confusion and fear. It was the latter emotion that clinched in my chest. Kerdik wasn't supposed to be afraid of anything. What hope was there that any of us could stand against something that scared the most powerful being in all of Avalon?

My emerald dress was pooled on the floor around us as I clutched him tight. When his breathing started to even out, I nearly cried from the relief. "Honey, what is it? Kerdik?" I ran my hand over his chest, hoping to calm either one of us.

"Rosie?" he whispered, his eyes wide and worried.

"What happened? We were talking, then the palace started shaking, then you grabbed your chest like you're having a heart attack, and now... What? Are you hurt?"

I didn't know how much more weird Avalon stuff I could handle. Kerdik had just admitted to me that the ring he'd put on my finger when we'd first met held all of the lost magic in Faîte – both the good stuff and the bad. The ability to turn Fae into Vampires and werewolves had been locked away, along with other, less devastating magic, like the ability to fly or turn yourself invisible. The higher magic had been locked away when it was clear it was doing more harm than good. No one knew what became of it, except for Kerdik, who'd been waiting for someone he trusted to come along. All this time, an atomic bomb of magic had been perched on my ring finger.

"Something's happened to..." Kerdik's pupils flicked from side to side in alarm. He appeared as though he was seeing a scene far away that I couldn't witness.

And then suddenly, I could. Kerdik was in distress, so our connection made me see what he saw. The first time this happened, I'd seen through his eyes. Now it seemed I was seeing the world through his mind's eye.

Brìghde was on all fours, teeth gritted as she clutched at the stone floor of a dungeon with her mannish hands. Her pale skin and red hair were filthy. Her dress looked like it was pure earth – made of moss or something – and it was torn at the hem up to her knee. Her face was burned, but worse than pain, one of her cheeks and her forehead were now disfigured. The puckered and shiny skin was immoveable as she spoke. "Ye don't know what you've done, mortal! Once I break free of whatever it is you've got tha's holding me, I'll take my time tearing ye apart. Whatever protection ye have tha kept me from killing ye, I'll find a way around, make no mistake."

The focus shifted upward, and I saw before I heard the cruelty of my birth mother. Morgan le Fae was standing over Brìghde with a sneer that looked well-practiced. She wore a red satin gown with no bustle, her chocolate-colored hair tied up in a crown of braids. Her pinched nose matched mine, though her face looked so murderous, I wished none of my features matched hers. "That was a nice little surprise. I can't be killed by an immortal, eh? Why, if only I'd known earlier. The fun I could've had." She kicked Brìghde in the ribs, and Brìghde exhaled a puff of black smoke. "Now, summon him."

"I wouldn't wish you on Kerdik, and I wish a fair many grave depravities on him. Summon him yourself."

Morgan picked up the hat Kerdik had given me to wear back when we'd first met. When I'd been thrown into the well, my belongings had been left in Morgan's castle, leaving the Newsies cap up for grabs. "I've got a token from him, so you can use that to call him here."

"Call him yourself!"

"Why my acid doesn't control your will, I can't understand. At least your abilities have been weakened. I can't be killed by you, but I wonder if *you* can be killed by *me*?"

Kerdik and I both shouted for Morgan to stop when she set down the hat on the floor of the dungeon and picked up a knife. Our cries were ineffectual as Morgan picked up Brìghde by her hair and stabbed her through the chest.

Brìghde's howl had a hawk-like shriek to it, making my spine tingle. For a moment, she went limp, and Morgan released her to slump to the floor. I called out her name, but we were on opposite ends of the country. I could hear pounding and shouting, but those noises were in my immediate reality – no doubt Urien or Bastien realizing we were walled inside the bedroom, and trying to bust through the thick stone. Some people just lock the door when they want a little privacy, but not Kerdik. He'd erected stone to cover the door and window, so we could have a few moments uninterrupted.

I hadn't been expecting him to propose – to ask instead of demand I spend my second life with him. Neither of us expected me to say yes, but here we were, trapped in my bedroom while the world fell to pieces.

Brìghde began to stir, and my heart nearly stuttered. I didn't know Brìghde, but her lifeline was the same eternal circle as Kerdik's. If something could kill her, it might take him down, as well. Brìghde coughed out a raspy, "Harder next time, ye rotten bitch."

"Oh, I can make it hurt far worse than that."

"Pain doesn't mean the same to an immortal as it does to ye. Even what you've done to my face will heal."

"That would be true, if I didn't have pools more of it, ready to dowse you as soon as you get your bearings back. I'll have you here for as long as it takes to get what I need."

"Ye can't have it. It's a myth. I can't make ye immortal."

I paled, wishing anything else had come from her mouth. Morgan somehow knew about my extended lifespan now. She knew, and she wanted. It was the ultimate power – to remain on her throne forever, to be the second immortal to reign over Avalon.

Morgan's fist shook around her bejeweled dagger. "I know that Rosalie's immortal now! Only Kerdik, you or Cailleach could've made her that way, and I know it was Kerdik. He turned fool for her long ago." She stabbed Brìghde through the back, puncturing her lung. Her fury made it seem like she wasn't just angry at Brìghde, but that she meant the knife for me, whom she couldn't get at. Morgan spoke above Brìghde's gasp and scream. "If he can turn Rosalie immortal, then you can grant me that same favor! Do it, or your long life will be spent in my dungeon, howling like an animal." When Brìghde couldn't answer because of her punctured lung, Morgan huffed, as if her prisoner was being annoying on purpose. She tapped her foot impatiently as she waited for the wound to heal enough for their tumultuous back and forth. "I must warn you; if you don't give me what I need, I'll trap Kerdik here next. Don't think I won't do it. I'm not afraid of him!"

Only I knew how very untrue that declaration was.

Once Brìghde's injury closed up enough for her to

breathe, she growled out a venomous, "If ye cross Kerdik, it'll be the last thing ye do. What a sweet sight it'll be to watch ye fall."

"But he can't kill me. If you can't, then I'm certain I've become too powerful for his tricks. I thought he simply didn't care what I did to Avalon, but all this time, he was powerless to stop me." She picked up Kerdik's Newsies cap and twirled it in her hands. "Perhaps I'll lure Kerdik here with the same sort of mental torture that brought you to my doorstep." Morgan's laugh had a dark edge to it that made my spine stiffen with the chills. "Poor, poor Brìghde. You should know better than to take a human lover."

Brìghde's eyes sparked with angry tears. "Tha ye still draw breath means Kerdik knows he can't kill ye. I don't care what it takes; I'll find a way to tear your heart out, so I can feast on it at the Moon's Festival for all your enemies and followers to see. I'll end ye for what ye did to my Gilliam!"

Morgan laughed – a shrill, rueful sound. "Ah, yes. Your sweet love. You haven't taken a lover since Lugh, and that was when I was just a girl. It's good to break the heart every few decades. It reminds you where your weaknesses lie." Morgan strolled around the dungeon as if Brìghde hadn't just threatened her. "Now, do you think Kerdik will be more moved to come for my daughter if he thinks she's dead, or if he thinks she's injured? I know he wouldn't come to save you." Morgan spat on Brìghde's head, and I could practically feel her radiating with fury at being chained to the floor and treated like a dog. She leaned over and held the hat in front of Brìghde for her to sniff. "Use this to send our dear green friend a vision. I know you can do that. I saw Kerdik reach Urien decades ago like this."

"I don't know what this Rosalie looks like, so I can't send him an image, ye twit."

Morgan frowned and pulled out a paper from a book that was sitting atop a table that held various torture devices. I winced at the sight of the metallic and jagged instruments. "This is a sketch her *soumettre* drew up during his time in her bed. Use this."

I gasped as I saw Demi's careful drawing. It was me, but distorted. I was... I was beautiful in the black sketch, my hair curled perfectly across my pillow as I slept. To Demi, I looked like an angel, the sheet stretched taut across my breasts and a sweet dream making my features docile. My heart ached at the thought of Demi, and I hated Morgan for rifling through his things and using them against me like this.

Morgan moved Brìghde's bloody hand to Kerdik's abandoned cap and urged her on. "Summon him here, and I'll let you go. If he's in my castle, then Rosalie will be unprotected. I need her here. I need her Compass if I'm to find the higher magic and put it to good use."

Brìghde spat in Morgan's face, but steadied herself to comply. Her eyes closed, and an incomprehensible murmur flowed from her blistered lips.

I fell onto my butt as Brìghde's voice filled my head.

"Kerdik, stay far away from Morgan le Fae. Take your doll somewhere safe, and send Cailleach to rescue me. I can't save myself. There's an army of acid-enhanced soldiers marching on your Province 10 this very moment! Morgan's sending them to kill the civilians and capture this Rosalie person. She thinks your doll can find where Avalon's lost magic went to, because of her Compass birth blessing. Morgan wants more power, and is tired of chasing after the Jewels of Good Fortune. Go! I've seen the bodies in this dungeon. This is what will happen to your Rosalie if Morgan le Fae gets her hands on your doll! This is what she did to my Gilliam!"

An image too graphic to compute flooded my senses, making me cry out. I couldn't even make out the face of the man, so mangled was his entire body. His arm was twisted in a funny way, an eyeball and his nose were missing, and the black hair was matted with blood. His mouth was frozen open in a perpetual scream, which no doubt had been his last utterance to the universe. There was something familiar about his face, but it was so covered with blood, I couldn't examine the inkling too closely.

The image of the man faded, and was quickly replaced by the drawing of me come to life. Demi had sketched me sleeping peacefully, but the animated version had me missing an eye, blood pouring down my face, and a scream frozen on my lips. I was a macabre cartoon in black and white. A sketched dagger plunged into my chest, wrenching a terrified scream from me. It was the worst movie ever, and I was the star.

Kerdik's hand reached out and landed on mine, clutching it so we didn't lose each other in this altered state of reality.

Brìghde's warning was clear, and boomed so loud in my ears that I winced. "Take this Rosalie away somewhere safe and call Cailleach. I'll get her to lift your curse if ye tell my sister to rescue me!"

Kerdik gasped, holding tight to my hand as the graphic image of my defeated body faded, leaving us staring at the stone wall in my bedroom.

2

THE TERRIBLE PLAN

"No," Kerdik ruled, ignoring the men who were shouting at us to let them inside as he stood to address me. "I'll not involve Cailleach. If she falls, Éireland has no one."

I started gesturing animatedly with my hands, as I often did when people brought me a crazy idea and had the nerve to call it a plan. "But if you fall, then Avalon's on its own! Same argument, pal. Try again."

Kerdik scoffed at the audacity that I thought anything could make him fall. "Oh, darling. That you doubt me is always so surprising. I'll get Brìghde out without any harm coming to me."

"And then what? Morgan will always have another plan, another way of trying to control you. She's got an immortal locked in a dungeon, you dummy! You're not going anywhere near her castle."

Kerdik reared back, looking at me with a mixture of offense and mild amusement. "Did you truly just call me a dummy?"

I pinched the bridge of my nose, deflating. "I'm sorry. That was uncalled for. Totally mean of me. But still no. You can't go there."

Bastien and Urien had sledgehammers, it seemed, and were ramming them against the stone to try and break through. Kerdik rolled his eyes. "Oh, honestly. Can I not have a moment of privacy?"

"Here's a helpful tip: you'll probably get them to leave you alone if you don't lock yourself in a room with me during a supernatural earthquake."

"I didn't do that! It was an effect of Brìghde's distress. The immortals connect like that in dire circumstances, like how you can see through my eyes when I'm suffering."

I touched Kerdik's shoulder to get him to focus. "Can you let me out of here? I need to go to the castle."

"You're in a castle."

"Not here. Morgan's home, I meant. I have to go finish this."

Kerdik scoffed in my face, as if the very idea that I could be useful was preposterous. "Obviously not. You'll remain locked in this stone prison until I return after freeing Brìghde."

"How exactly are you going to do that? Morgan's got some crazy mojo that can render immortals useless! Like it or not, you can't end Morgan." My eyes flickered with fear at the words that tumbled out of my mouth. "You can't kill her, but I can. I'm a Daughter of Avalon, Kerdik. We can't fall by the hands of anyone, except for another Daughter of Avalon. I can end this. I can end the madness for all of us."

Kerdik's mouth fell open, angry and shocked that this was my plan. "No. No, and never! Morgan will never lay eyes on you again."

Hurt slashed through my heart at the terrible conversation we were stuck in. "You're only thinking about me; you're not thinking about all of Avalon. Don't you understand that this is bigger than us? If Morgan isn't stopped, she'll find a way to end Brìghde. Then it's eternal winter in Éireland, if I'm predicting correctly, since Brìghde has the power to usher in the spring. If Morgan can lure and trap Brìghde, then what's to say she won't do the same to Cailleach or to you? Avalon needs you, Kerdik!"

"No, they need *you*. You're the one who's brought peace to the nation. You're the one they left their oppression in Province 1 for. They got along without me just fine for two decades. Now that I'm back, there's full-on war."

"Um, hello, that was happening when you were gone, too. Province 10 has a chance now."

"Because of you! You're the one who thought of the aqueducts. It's you and Lane who united more than half the kingdom and set them free from Morgan's tyranny." Kerdik reached out and fingered one of my curls, staring at it with longing. "If Morgan kills the Avalon Rose, what is there left to fight for? You're the symbol they've left their homes for, fought for and died for. You'll not hand yourself over to death so easily. You'd be slaughtering the hopes and dreams of the hundreds of thousands who only realized their freedom because you fought for it."

I drew in a steadying breath. "Look, I'm not seeing many options, here. It's either me, Lane or my cousin Gwen who can pull the trigger on Morgan."

"Gwen's not a blood daughter of Avalon. She was adopted."

"Okay. That leaves Lane, who's too jacked up to make the trek. It's got to be me, and you know it."

Kerdik glared at me, his nostrils flaring at my logic, which was pretty solid. "No."

"I don't need your permission. I'm giving you a heads-up."

Kerdik moved to where the door used to be, and pressed his palm to the stone. The rocks grew thicker and more impenetrable, bubbling out as if to mock me. "You'll stay in here until I say so, which will be after I've rescued Brìghde. Morgan will get her own little stone prison in her castle, so she's nice and contained, and can't cause more trouble."

"Right, because that's all it would take. She can't cast spells from inside a room. She can't murmur incantations. Come on, Kerdik! She's clearly got magic you don't even know about, if she can trap and strip the power from an immortal!"

Kerdik's anger rose to a shout. "You'll not throw yourself into harm's way for a country you plan on leaving! I don't know what patience you imagine I possess, but you'll find a new topic before I lose my temper."

"This is you holding onto your temper? Stop throwing a fit and think logically, you big baby!"

"You're being a child!"

"You're being controlling!"

"Because you're suicidal if you think this is a good plan!"

"I'll go!" came a female voice from the other side of the wall. It was only then I realized that the sledgehammers had stopped trying to tear down the wall, and my plan wasn't the only one that could be entertained.

3

OVER MY DEAD BODY

y head whipped around to stare at the stone. "Lane? You didn't hear anything. Go back to bed."

"Don't you use that tone with me, girlfriend," Lane spouted back with attitude. I could practically see her head swiveling like the valley girl she sometimes was.

My neck shrank at being corrected by my mom, but Kerdik postured. "Excellent idea, Duchess." He waved his hand, and the stone blockade disappeared.

Bastien tumbled inside, his face sweaty and his expression surly. I thought he might put down the hammer he'd been trying to break the wall with, but he charged forward and took a swing at Kerdik's head.

Kerdik held his hand up, mutating the hammer into a bouquet of flowers that bashed him over the head. Hard and thick vines sprouted from the stone floor where the petals fell, and wrapped around Bastien's wrists, tugging him down to his knees. "Tell me why I shouldn't tear your head off right now," Kerdik asked, miffed.

"You don't lock yourself in a room with my fiancée ever again!"

I pressed my hand to Kerdik's puffed chest, and my dad moved into the room to stand in front of Bastien. "You'll not harm Rosalie's fiancé, Kerdik. If you did, she would never forgive you."

Kerdik scoffed incredulously. "Oh, but he's allowed to take a swing at me?"

Bastien was fuming. "As many swings as it takes to knock some sense into you! Stay away from Rosie!"

Kerdik's hand started out between my shoulders, and then slowly sloped downward to take up the coveted space on the small of my back. He cast Bastien a superior smile just to make him rage. "Go on out into the hallway, darling."

I scoffed at the scene and clapped my hands to diffuse the fight. "Everyone, chill! Bigger things are going on right now. Morgan's got Brìghde, and she's lost a fair amount of her power. Maybe all of it except her immortality. She can't get out of Morgan's trap."

Kerdik released Bastien from his hold, and quickly laid out our vision after the gasps settled. "I'll be leaving to see if I can't rescue her and set Morgan straight." Kerdik looked around to my dad, Bastien, Lane, and now Reyn and Draper, sighing that so many people would now know a treasured secret he'd only told a few about. "Only a Daughter of Avalon can kill a Daughter of Avalon. If another person tries, it doesn't work. It was a failsafe Urien asked me to put in place back when he was in love with his wife. Morgan vexed me too often, so he asked me to put a protection on her against my magic."

"A mistake on my part, for certain," Dad allowed with a contrite downward tilt of his head. "Rosalie's right; Morgan needs to be put down. I don't relish the thought of it, but Avalon has suffered enough."

"Good. It's settled. I'll see you all when we get back." I raised my chin in defiance, but my dad shook his head in time with everyone else in the room.

Lane spoke for the group. "I'll go. I wouldn't lose a wink of sleep over ending my sister. I won't put that on your conscience."

I rolled my eyes. "You don't actually sleep, so that grand declaration's all hyperbole, you know. I'm going. You're still not at one hundred percent, and this needs to get taken care of now."

Lane met Kerdik's eyes, her posture straight and queenly. "You say you love my daughter?"

Kerdik straightened and met Lane's gaze with the resolve of a promise. "I do."

Bastien fumed, but remained quiet at my side.

Lane nodded. "Good. Then you'll protect Rosie from all of this. Take me to Morgan, and let me end this for Avalon."

Reyn's fist tightened, and he stepped forward to stand at Lane's side. "Where you go, I go."

Draper moved to her other side, posturing like the prince he was. "Same for me. I'll help Lane get to Morgan."

"Over my dead body, Lane!" I shook my head, frustrated. "No, guys! This is my fight. It's me she wants, so I'll be the one ending it."

Lane's tone softened when she turned to me. "Honey, if it's you Morgan wants, then you're the one person we can't let her near. Don't you see that?"

"You're barely upright!" I pointed out, wishing I didn't have to hurt her pride to make her see reason. "How can you not see what a terrible idea this is?"

Lane ignored me and turned to my dad. "I'll need my sword, and armor for all three of us." She gripped Kerdik's hand, though I could see her visible discomfort at being so near to him. "Thank you. We'll gather our things and be ready in ten minutes."

Kerdik nodded. "See that you are. I don't fancy waiting a second longer than we have to." His gaze flicked to my dad's. "Morgan's army's all been doused with her acid that makes the soldiers stronger and bend completely to her will. They're marching on Province 10 as we speak. They have orders to kill your people and take your daughter to Morgan. I'll do what I can in the next ten minutes to fortify your city, but beyond that, you're on your own."

My dad moved in to grip Kerdik in a hug I could tell my bestie needed, but would never ask for. "Thank you, old friend. Thank you for sparing my daughter. Please take care of my sister while she's with you. The Lost Duchess is the last respectable one in all of Avalon. We cannot lose her."

My dad was more than willing to let Lane throw herself to the she-wolf rather than let me try my capable hand at saving our province. I grumbled at the injustice of it all, but no one paid me any mind.

Kerdik nodded solemnly. "As you wish it, old friend."

"Stop this!" I shouted, angry that a whole plan was happening without me being able to lift a finger to help.

My dad turned away to go after Lane. "I'll see they have all they need, then I'll ready the soldiers."

"Wait, Dad! I'm coming with you. I'll help you with the soldiers."

Urien turned and embraced me, planting a kiss to my forehead. "I love you, my dear. All these years, I never dreamed I'd be so fortunate as to have such a fiercely loyal daughter to claim as my own."

"I love you, too."

Then Urien's eyes left mine and looked over my shoulder with a nod. He stepped back just as Kerdik's arm banded and then tightened around my waist. At first, it was a gentle hug that was more affectionate than I knew we could be in public. When my dad stepped away to follow Lane and the others, the hug became a restraining hold. "Stay with her, Bastien," my Dad said over his shoulder as he turned the corner and left me with the two bulls.

I struggled against Kerdik, but if you can believe it, the immortal superhuman was stronger than me. "Let me go! My dad needs help out there."

Kerdik shushed me, leaning down to whisper in my ear. "Tell me you wouldn't lock the people you love in a tower to keep them from harm. We are the same monster."

My eyes widened in alarm as I screamed. "No! Kerdik, don't!"

Kerdik pointed his free hand toward the door, and filled in the gaps with fresh stone, letting me go once there was no way I could escape.

4

KERDIK'S MOMENT OF WEAKNESS

Kerdik ignored my fists on the rock wall and turned a deaf ear to my howls for help. He soundlessly moved over to my tub so he could fill it with water. He didn't bother talking to me, since I was busy cussing him out, but instead addressed Bastien, who was the only other person in the room. "There's enough water in here to last you both a few days. I'll bring you some food before I leave, too. You'll keep her in here until the water runs out, and then you can bash your way out with this hammer." He started molding a heavy sledge-hammer out of fresh rock that morphed out from his palm like playdough.

Bastien nodded, surprisingly levelheaded about the whole incarceration thing once he'd been released from the vines that had restrained him. "Works for me. Thanks for this. You're right that Morgan's gunning for Rosie. She needs her for something, though I don't know what."

Kerdik blew out a breath and spoke in a rush, pushing all the words out so he could get out quickly. "Morgan figured out that Rosie's still got her Compass ability. She wants to use it to find Avalon's lost magic."

Bastien rolled his eyes. "If Rosie could do that, she already would've. She can't track something nebulous like that. She tracks people, objects. Morgan makes me crazy. Be sure that Lane makes her suffer."

Kerdik ignored my scowl and took my hand, jerking it so Bastien could see my ring. "Rosie doesn't need to track it, because I gave it to her a while ago. In this ring is Avalon's lost magic, and Éireland's."

Bastien's hand went over his mouth to stifle his howl of shock. "Are you kidding me with this? We've been walking around with the power to turn the Fae into any number of incurable monsters? Maybe that's something you should've told us! What if we'd accidentally set the magic loose? What then? Then Faîte's crawling with creatures we can't escape because you couldn't be bothered to keep such a dangerous thing away from the people!"

I didn't understand why Kerdik looked actually proud of Bastien's outrage until he replied in a cool, calm voice. "You understand how dangerous this magic would be if restored to the lands, then. That's good. Some just see more magic as a good thing, and don't care to think through the consequences."

"Get it off her! Take it back!"

"Only she and I can take it off her finger without suffering dire consequences. Rosie can be trusted to guard the magic. She can't access it, anyway. It was becoming too tempting for me, so I knew I had to get it out of my hands."

"Get that ring off her finger, Kerdik! Take it and destroy it!"

Kerdik shook his head. "It's not that simple. Destroying the ring would only set the magic loose in Faîte all over again. You can't destroy magic; you can only mutate it. Containing it is the only way. I'm telling you all this because if something should happen to me, I want you to guard Rosie as if the safety of both Avalon and Éireland depend on it."

Bastien ran his fingers though his hair, overwhelmed. "Who else knows about this?"

"Brìghde knows Rosie has the lost magic, but not that it's in her ring. Brìghde and Cailleach helped me trap it all, but I hid it away so they wouldn't be tempted to set it all loose again. It's safer this way. No one else can know. Cailleach can't be trusted with it, because she'll try to sort out the good from the bad, which can't be done. It's what she wanted to do years ago when we were working to round it all up. All higher magic has to be put away. Callie might not see reason with that, and I don't want to risk it." Kerdik frowned. "I can only hope Brìghde hasn't told her sister that Rosie's got the lost magic."

"You're telling me *the* Cailleach might come after

Rosie? You expect me to be able to defend her against immortals?"

Kerdik lowered his chin and leaned in conspiratorially. "Look, back when I first met you and enhanced your body, I knew you would protect Rosie. Do you recall when I broke down your body and repaired it, so you would be worthy of the post of being Rosie's *Guardien*?"

"Vaguely," Bastien seethed with bitterness dripping from his tone.

"I made it so that an immortal can't kill you. It's what saved you from death at my own hand on many occasions."

Bastien's eyebrow quirked, and he stood up straighter. "You're telling me I can't be killed?"

"You can be killed, just not by an immortal. I enhanced you the day I gave Rosie her ring. You were to protect her, sure, but you're also protecting the lost magic of Avalon and Éireland."

Bastien's hand went over his mouth, unable to process all of it with any sort of grace. "Kerdik, man. If I would've known, I..."

"You'd protect her with the same ferocity you do now. That you fell in love with her? Well, I certainly can't fault you for that. Keep her safe." Then, in a brotherly move neither of us expected, Kerdik reached out and clutched Bastien's shoulder. "Keep Avalon safe."

"I promise," Bastien said with a firm nod.

Kerdik turned to where the window used to be and

clicked his fingers, making the stones over the glass tumble to the floor with several bowling ball-sounding cracks. He popped open the window and surveyed the land with furrowed eyebrows. "If I faint, do see that I don't tumble out the window," he said over his shoulder to us. "That would be so embarrassing."

I let out a noise of distress. "Jeez! What are you up to that would make you faint, Kerdik?"

"Protecting what's mine. I worked for a long time with your little friend Judah to get the aqueducts just the right dimensions. I won't see an army come and mess up my handiwork."

I smirked at him. "Admit it. You love Avalon. You want to watch over us."

Kerdik shook his head. "I want to watch over *you*."

Bastien grumbled several curses under his breath, letting me know their little truce was reaching its breaking point.

Kerdik blew out a long breath, and then lifted his hands, stretching them out of the window. I moved to his side, and Bastien peeked over my shoulder to watch the sight that ripped a gasp from us both. Stone walls shot up from the earth, building on the one we'd been constructing with the sweat of our hands. Kerdik took our handiwork and made it taller, thicker and infinitely longer. The wall snaked on down the edge of the territory, until I couldn't see its end anymore.

"What are you doing?" I asked, breathless at the

incredible feats of nature Kerdik could manipulate. Sure, I could've guessed he was capable of such grandeur, but to see it in action was a whole other thing. My eyes were as wide as saucers as my vision picked up the wall circling back to us, enclosing Province 10 in a protective three-foot thick wall that looked to be about twenty feet tall.

It was then I realized that Kerdik was shaking. His hands dropped and gripped the window's sill, his biceps trembling to keep his body upright. "Stop!" I cried, my arms going around his middle to make sure he didn't collapse. "Kerdik, no more!"

But just like Kerdik's love, his abilities were always grander than I could predict. In the same trail the construction of the wall had gone, the earth began to dig itself out along the outer edge of the wall, about a foot out from the stone.

"Moats," Bastien marveled, amazed at Kerdik's prowess to think things through in such complete and militaristic fashion. The moats Kerdik dug with his mind were seven feet wide, and looked too deep for a man to stand in. The well for the moats went quicker around the perimeter of the whole province, most likely because that involved moving the earth that was already there, and not manufacturing deep stone walls from scratch.

"Kerdik, you're going to hurt yourself! The wall is enough to keep us safe. You can stop!"

Kerdik ignored me, his focus sharp as a laser. He was gritting his teeth, and I saw sweat beading on his forehead.

When the moat was dug and stretched all the way around the stone wall, Kerdik let out a cry of anguish, and I saw water filling up in the deep divots. He was in physical pain, and after this he had to go fight a battle filled with powerful magic and immortals.

"Kerdik, stop! The province will be safe!" When he didn't stop, I wedged myself between him and the window, pressing my hands to his cheeks so he could see only my face. "I'll be safe," I promised, knowing in the depths of my heart that would be the only thing he needed to hear.

Kerdik collapsed in my arms, his eyelids closing as the sun went out behind me in a blink. I let out a noise of fear, but Bastien helped me lower Kerdik to the ground in the dark without letting him fall. The cries of the people below us outside reached my ears, but I had bigger problems. I sat next to Kerdik's head, holding his hand as angst dominated my features.

"I'll get some water," Bastien offered, putting aside his feud with Kerdik to be helpful. I loved him so much in that moment, adoring the wonderful man who could see the bigger picture through his personal opinions.

Bastien flicked water on Kerdik's face and slapped his cheeks a few times before Kerdik roused, bringing the sunshine with him. Light filtered in through the window, shining on the men I loved without hesitation.

"Rosie?" Kerdik's voice sounded sleepy, like he was speaking through a fog.

"I told you to stop!" I yelled, upset and scared. "You did

too much and you fainted! Actual fainting, Kerdik. I'm so mad at you right now, I can barely feel relieved you're alright."

The corner of Kerdik's mouth lifted in tired amusement. "You love me."

Bastien went from elated to pissed. "Listen, guy on the floor, I'll knock you right out if you keep up that kinda talk."

"Help me up?" Kerdik asked, sounding pitiful and weak.

I only helped him to sit, knowing it would be foolish if he tried his hand at standing. My arms wrapped around his torso, hugging him to me and letting his chin loop over my shoulder. "Never again, do you hear me? You need me alive? I need you in one piece!"

His lips moved against my ear with a gentle, "I love you, too." Then he cleared his throat and stretched out his back. "I'm alright. It's just cramming all that magic in one shot that gets a little taxing."

"Why didn't you do that months ago when we first moved here?" Bastien accused. "Rosie's been working on that wall with the men forever."

"Yes, and it brought the people together. Gave them a common goal. Plus, Rosie said it was good for her to be doing manual labor. Therapeutic or something, if I recall correctly."

I gaped at him, standing to help Bastien pull him up. "You do care about Avalon."

"Never doubt that I do. If I'd come along and done this the first day, there wouldn't have been the camaraderie your people needed to be able to stick together when things grew difficult. Now they'll fight alongside each other, putting aside the grudges of their previous provincial allegiances so they can be one." Kerdik leaned heavily on us both, so we led him slowly toward the chair in the corner of the room, one stumbling foot after the other.

I frowned at him, taking in his head that had a hard time staying level. "You overdid it, old man. Now you're benched, do you hear me? Lane and them can ride on horses to get to Morgan. You're sitting this one out."

Kerdik looked over at me as if I'd said something funny. "Aw, that's sweet. Are you trying to take care of me?"

"Shut up!" I screeched, my nerves utterly fried when his foot tripped again, and we had to steady him from falling. "This isn't sweet. This is me yelling at you for jeopardizing your health. This is me tearing you a new one because you shouldn't push yourself to the limit like that!"

I was about to protest the whole plan in general with plenty of outraged hand gestures, but Kerdik suddenly dropped his arm from around Bastien's shoulder and jerked me to him right before we could lower him to his chair. He planted a firm kiss to my lips, unapologetic to Bastien or me, unashamed of the connection we'd tried to sever too many times to count. Before Bastien could punch him, Kerdik waved his hand, and vines sprang up from the floor once again to keep Bastien from intruding on his moment. I was embarrassed and nervous, so I pressed my hands to his chest and tried to push Kerdik away. "Stop it!"

"Just another second, darling," he promised, sucking on my lower lip while Bastien howled at us. Something prickly touched my tongue, and then leapt into me. I stumbled back when Kerdik released me, choking on something I couldn't cough out.

"What was that? What did you do to me?" I yelled, angry that he'd kissed me in front of Bastien, and that he'd done something magical in the process without discussing it with me first.

"It's just a little locating charm that will help me find my way back to you."

I glared at him. "Did you have to kiss me to do the charm?"

"Of course not." Kerdik merely smirked at us both, ignoring my gasp of outrage. "I'll come back for you, darling," he vowed, and then he sealed in the window with a thick layer of stone, encasing us in the darkness. Without another word, Kerdik vanished from my bedroom.

5

THE TEASE AND THE TERROR

It took us a solid five minutes of stumbling around in the dark basically reenacting the Three Stooges before Bastien and I were able to locate the lantern on the wall. When dim light fell on our faces, we didn't speak for a solid twenty seconds. Two entire television commercials could've come and gone in the span of our weighted silence. Bastien's expression was firm, and when he finally spoke, his voice carried a deep strength to it that communicated he would be the one with the upper hand. "Are you in love with him?" He winced, and then covered my mouth. "Don't answer that. Anything you say will just make me angry at you, because I know the truth. I know you're in love with him. For as long as he's been pursuing you, I can't say I'm surprised." He stared hard into my eyes, his caramel boring into my respective blue and peach irises.

I moved Bastien's hand away with a slight shake of my head. "I don't want to fight with you about this. I have two lifespans to think about. I made it clear to Kerdik that I'd be spending this one with you. I'll catch up with him in my second life."

"Make it clearer," Bastien countered. "Make it so clear that he doesn't try to kiss you anymore."

"I can do that." I sank into the embrace I worried might feel different with Kerdik's locator charm in me, but there we were… still us.

He frowned, picking up my hand to examine my finger. "Well played on his part. He put a ring on your finger the day he met you. It's what I should've done."

"I think kidnapping me and drugging my best friend is a sweet way to get to the altar. Think of the stories we'll tell our kids someday of how mommy and daddy first met."

The corner of Bastien's mouth lifted. "Kids, eh? I wouldn't mind a couple of those. When we're in Common, that is. I practically have a heart attack every time anyone comes near you in Avalon. I can't imagine adding worrying about my kids on top of that." His eyes widened. "Whoa. I just said the phrase 'my kids'. Spooky."

"I think I might like spooky. When I'm a little older. I don't think I can handle that kind of responsibility at the moment."

"Right. It's nothing like ruling a kingdom. That's cake compared to children."

"Thanks for being you. You're the best you I know." I yawned, but tried to keep my indiscretion to myself.

Bastien pointed to my bed with a strict expression. "Finally. I'm exhausted. I didn't want to be the first one to cave."

"How can you sleep with an impending war just outside our city?"

"Easy. They're not here yet, and there's nothing I can do to fend them off. You're my number one job, and I can do that here, in the comfort of this stone prison."

"Nicest jail cell I've ever been in, that's for sure."

Bastien kicked his boots off and glanced over his shoulder to make sure the stone wall was still in place. He unbuttoned his flannel and yanked his undershirt over his head, peering over his shoulder again, as if afraid someone might see all his scars and think less of his gorgeous body.

I closed the gap between us and stroked his chest with my flat palms, easing his insecurity and letting him know I very much wanted the body he'd ended up with. I leaned up on my toes and kissed his lips, relishing the feel of the powerful man melting beneath my touch. I loved the way Bastien melted for me.

When he pulled back, he met my eyes with purpose as he unbuckled his belt and let his jeans drop to the floor. "Get in bed."

I thrilled at his request that came out like a command. I grabbed a lavender tank top and moved behind the parti-tion. My dress pooled at my ankles, my skin practically glowing as I slid the tank top over my head and rolled it down my torso. I looked down at my matching underwear and tank top, knowing that very soon, I would be far more naked with the man I loved, and who dared love me back.

When I stepped out from behind the divide, I was nervous, suddenly rethinking how nearly naked I was. My day-to-day work clothing was often dirty from laboring on the wall, or my dresses too princess-y to touch. This was my body, and the shape of me was unconcealed. It was a heady feeling to be so honest with my fiancé – to let him see me as I was.

Bastien's intake of breath was all the praise I needed. His wide eyes drank me in, memorizing each detail, every curve and nuance. "You... you can't wear that. Go put on one of my shirts or something. I can't... I'll never be able to sleep if you're curled up next to me, looking like that."

"Who said anything about sleep?" I replied with a hint of a coy tease to my tone.

Apparently, that was all the green light Bastien needed to hear. He cleared the gap between us in the span of a few long steps, laying a kiss on me so grand, I finally understood the phrase "weak in the knees." I swooned for him, my lashes fluttering shut as he lifted me up in his arms. My legs wrapped around his waist, pressing us together in ways that left little mystery between our nearly nude bodies. Bastien understood how to make me gasp for him; he knew how to make me come undone. His capable palm slapped my backside three times before he dumped me onto the bed, towering over me like he was a giant, and I was the Christmas feast he would be treating himself to.

Bastien took a step back to pace himself, gather up his game plan before he pounced and ravished. When he picked up my left foot, I wished for the savage in him to let loose and christen our engagement however he pleased. Instead, he took his time kissing and nibbling on the inside of my ankle. My nerve endings went into hyper-drive, so great was my anticipation of exactly this, and exactly him. My body twitched and writhed as he made his way up to the inside of my knee, not caring or even remembering the planet decorum was kept in. All I wanted was more of this, more of him.

Bastien didn't deny me. Finally leaning forward, he braced himself on his elbows to kiss me while he lowered his hips to mine. My knees were shaking as they fell open, inviting him – always inviting. His body was large and firm, and cliché though it might seem, his vicious side made me feel incredibly safe, tucked beneath him as I was. "Marry me," he breathed between kisses, meeting my eyes with lust and love.

"Yes." My reply was easy, and tumbled out of me without hesitation. I knew I was still young, but I'd lived through what felt like several whole lives already. We'd been through two worlds and multiple kingdoms together. After all the dust settled, there he was, coming undone atop me while I cursed the thin barriers between us. We were teenagers finally, making up for lost time, since neither of us had taken full advantage of the freedom and folly of our youth.

He met my eyes with purpose as he fingered the hem of my tank top, silently asking for permission, which I granted him with a tongue-laced kiss. Bastien took his time teasing the hem, rolling it up my torso with excruciating slowness, just to make us both crazy. Oh, how crazy I was for him. I was willing to put Kerdik aside, to cross Avalon to find Bastien, and pledge the rest of Bastien's lifespan only to him. Finally, finally I was ready to let my affections fall only to him. After all our back and forth, we were in the same place at the same time, looking into each other's eyes with something deeper than lust. It was a promise that we wouldn't lose our grip on the love we'd been lucky enough not to break with all our carelessness and pitfalls that had led us to this moment.

Bastien kissed the swell of my breasts through the thin material of my tank top right when he'd run out of stomach to expose. The line we were about to cross was significant, and we both felt its weight. He'd seen me naked before, but this was different. This was my choice, and we were wholly alone. I was in my right mind, ready to be driven to insanity by his capable ministrations.

When the candlelit room began to fade from my vision, I tried my best to hold onto the moment I'd waited so very long for. I wanted Bastien, but in the next breath, all I saw was my mother's face. Morgan laughed with cruelty as she kicked the body I was seeing through square in the ribs. I cried out in shock, hearing my own protest and Kerdik's.

The sexy moment was stolen away, leaving Bastien scrambling in confusion. Terror descended on all three of us, as Kerdik and I began cursing my mother, while we tried desperately to think of an escape.

6

GILLIAM THE PUPPET

Sexy time came to a screeching halt as Bastien sat me up on the bed and resituated my tank top, so we could both think clearly. He listened carefully to the one-sided conversation I was living out through Kerdik. I was just trying to keep up.

Morgan raised a hollowed-out horn that I guessed belonged to an animal like Dahu (a unicorn deer) over Kerdik's head. The worst part was her smile when the golden liquid oozed from the horn. She knew it would bite us with agony that only came from the sensation of skin melting. I screamed through Kerdik's pain. My hands went to my face to check for scarring, but I was still me. When Kerdik did the same, his fingers came away wrinkled and shiny with the beginnings of an acid burn. Anger roiled up in me when I felt Kerdik's fear. I wanted to avenge him, to scoop him up and whisk him away from the pain he was writhing through. But he was stuck, and thus, so was I.

I watched my mother's eyes shimmer with glee. Though I'd never seen that megalomaniac smile graze my face, I now knew what it would look like if I went full-on evil villain. "How does it feel to be powerless?" she needled him, dumping more acid atop his head. It sizzled as it dripped down his back.

I howled in time with Kerdik, feeling physical agony he'd not been accustomed to all that often in his elite life. "Enjoy this, Morgan. Enjoy every second of your victory. When I take it all away from you, I'll relish making you suffer every bit as much."

"Is that so? Is that what you intended for my baby sister to do to me? You wanted her to kill me?" She tsked him. "Pity Lane was so easy to spot. I've got this castle set with every warding charm you can possibly think of. I know the second an immortal crosses my doorstep, and as you can see, now I know how to defend my territory against your unwelcome advances."

Kerdik let out a groan through his torment. "What magic are you using that's making me so weak?"

I didn't actually expect her to answer, and rolled my eyes when Morgan replied with, "A little of this, a little of that. I needed the tears of an immortal, so I sent my dear Rigby to seduce your Brìghde. Rigby is the best. So loyal, so willing to please. Brìghde didn't take long before she fell for his charms. I can't blame the girl. He played the part of the weary Gilliam – a man who only needed the love of a strong woman to set him free." She set down the horn and turned, revealing Brìghde on all fours, chained to the stone dungeon's floor behind her. Morgan leaned over and cupped Brìghde's cheeks, as if she was a beloved pet, and cooed in her face. "Rigby's the best lover a woman can take into her bed. Poor, stupid Brìghde. You confessed so much to him, after blissful nights turned into tear-filled heart-to-hearts. He bottled your tears for me, because no matter how much you thought he loved you, Rigby's always belonged to me."

Morgan opened the cell door when a knock came, revealing none other than Rigby, unharmed and very much alive. Brìghde cried out her heartbreak at being so very had by this mere mortal. "I thought ye died! I saw your mangled body!"

"A mere illusion," Morgan explained, though Rigby was tight-lipped. He wore the same beige fitted pants, white dress shirt, and red jacket with gold threading. I drank in the sight of the friend I'd thought was mine, studying his long nose, the dark and wavy brown hair that curled up at the base of his neck like a forty-year-old Disney prince. His green eyes were closed off and gave nothing away. He could make you feel like he was your very best friend, and then throw you away because that was his job, and you were the trash that needed taking out.

He was ever the professional I remembered him to be, but it wasn't lost on me that he winced when he saw the state the bedraggled Brìghde had been reduced to. Just as I knew it broke his heart to obey, I knew he wouldn't lift a finger to save Brìghde, just as he hadn't lifted a finger to save me from being thrown down into the well.

Rigby kept his eyes on Morgan, his expression composed once again as he held the food tray in his hands. "Your dinner, your majesty most high."

I blanched at the greeting, wishing I could scrub that title out of my ears for all of eternity.

"Very good. How's my dear little sister?"

"Duchess Elaine of the Shamed Province 10 is secured in the lowest rung of the dungeon, just as you requested. Even if King Urien sends out a battalion to reclaim her, they'll never find the door to her cell."

"And the others? Reyn and Prince Draper?"

"Secured as well. In total darkness, as you commanded."

"Very good. I'll see to them when I've tired of these two."

I felt something rally in Kerdik, and heard him shout, "How long were you intending on keeping Urien in his slumber? Which immortal grew you the pure Hemlock that allowed you to control his life like that?"

I knew what he was doing, and wanted to hug him for it. He was drawing attention onto himself, so Morgan wouldn't grow tired of torturing him. Then she'd leave Lane alone until help came.

I was the help. There was no one else.

Kerdik pressed on, making his tone drip with obnoxious irritability, which I'm sure wasn't too difficult an acting job. "I don't understand how you drained my magic."

Morgan's smile was sinister, though it had a brush of sweetness to it that made her appear beautiful in her treachery. "Of course you don't. When I learned of your promise to Urien that only a Daughter of Avalon could kill a Daughter of Avalon – people confess the best secrets when in the process of succumbing to Hemlock – I knew I had to counter your blessing somehow. I couldn't very well best your magic, but I could build on it. I studied the Jewels of Good Fortune, collecting as many as I could from my sisters. Everyone thinks all I care about is keeping my land and people fertile, but that's not my only goal. They were fascinating trinkets, beaming out magic to the land. I started to wonder if I could reverse the pull, sucking magic inward, instead of having the jewels pour magic outward." Her eyes twinkled malevolently. "So I made myself become the treasure, drawing out the magic of others to store in my body, gaining power each time."

"You were always an excellent student," Kerdik said grudgingly.

"I made it so that if anyone tried to kill me, not only would they not succeed, thanks to you, but I made sure their magic would spill out of them." She frowned down at him. "Usually I can snatch it up and keep it for myself, but I can't manage to hold onto the immortal magic you two seem to ooze without thought. I'll figure it out eventually, though. I only had my sights set on Avalon, but to rule Éireland as well? Why limit my reach?" She leaned over and pinched Brighde's cheek, smiling as the woman on all fours growled like a feral beast. "This way, if my sisters do try to kill me, they'll lose their magic in the process."

Morgan really had thought of everything. I couldn't help but admire her carefully constructed web that so many had stumbled into.

My dad, Mad and Link were rallying the men to ready for a battle that was coming to us. They couldn't spare the men to ride out and rescue Lane. Even if they did, it didn't sound like they would be able to find her in that second, secret dungeon.

I tried not to panic at the thought of my Lane being kept somewhere in the dark. My anger absolutely seethed in my veins when I pictured Reyn down there, and even worse, my Draper.

I felt around until my hands touched something I couldn't see, feeling the prickly cheeks of the man whose face brought me home every time I looked into his eyes. When Morgan disappeared from my vision and Bastien filled my view, I stiffened and sat up. The account of everything I saw tumbled out of me in a rush as I ran to the wardrobe to tug on a pair of jeans, socks and shoes. "Come on!" I urged him when he looked at the jeans I shoved at him in confusion. "Let's bust out this stone wall and get to them!"

Bastien's stony face gave no misconceptions that he could be argued with. "No. Even Kerdik said that you're to be kept here until he comes back. I'm not breaking you out just to take you straight into the lion's den. Don't you understand how off the rails Morgan is?"

"My family's being held in her dungeon! Two immortals might die, Bastien! Don't you get what that could do to Faîte?"

"I understand, but it doesn't change the fact that you've got a ring that could undo pretty much everything we know about Faîte if Morgan got her hands on it. If she can control Kerdik, then she can find a way to get that ring off your finger and use what's in there for her own gain. It's our one advantage, Ro. You're talking about strolling into a place that's rigged for detecting powerful magic."

I stepped back, angry, but unwilling to argue further. Pacing the room, I thought through all the ways I could bust myself out of here. "I could nab a horse and ride to Morgan's castle. Of course, I'd most likely be running straight into Morgan's army, which would be super inconvenient."

"To say the least. Are you really trying to find a way around this?"

"It's like you just met me. Of course I am. I'm not going to sit up here and wait it out while my friends and my family are in danger. If only there was a way to zap myself from this room to Morgan's castle."

"And then what? How could you possibly get them out and best Morgan on her own turf?"

I shook my head. "One problem at a time."

"If you try to kill Morgan, all your magic will spill out."

I shrugged. "I don't use my magic. I'm the perfect candidate for this. I'm a Daughter of Avalon, and I don't care if my magic spills out for anyone to scoop up. Let her listen to the healers she tried to shut up."

Bastien shook his head. "That's if you can even get past her guards, past her wards, and then manage to win in hand-to-hand combat. Those are significant setbacks, Ro."

I waved off his warnings and rolled my eyes. "Blah, blah, blah. That's not the winning attitude I was hoping for. I already know the problems. Help me find the solutions."

Bastien crossed his arms over his chest. "Did I ever tell you this is one of your least appealing sides? The one that says, 'blah, blah, blah' to my completely legitimate warnings does nothing for me. You're being stubborn!"

I whirled on him and jabbed my finger toward the bed. "The sooner we get everyone home, the sooner we can get back down to business. How's that for motivation?"

Bastien smirked at me and slid on his jeans, buckling them up and slipping his undershirt over his head. "I'm sufficiently invested now. Okay, problem one is that we can't get past Morgan's wards."

"Who can't? I mean, it doesn't sound like Lane's the one

who tripped the alarm. It sounds like they came in with Kerdik, who triggered the wards."

Bastien nodded. "Okay. But Kerdik gave you extra magic, plus that double lifespan. That might do something."

"Crap. You're right." My eyebrows furrowed, frustrated that I couldn't get past that problem. "We'll put a pin in that one for now."

"We still have to make it past Morgan's guards."

I slapped my stomach. "I can do that, if I'm focusing enough. I can ask my internal Compass to lead me away from her spies. Easy-peasy."

"I was hoping for a plan that was easy-peasy." He buttoned up his flannel, sighing at the thin, tight tank top that highlighted my PG-13 parts. "When we go away for our honeymoon, I don't care what happens in Avalon, I'm working those clothes off you, and they're staying off you for a solid week."

I smirked up at him, stepping closer so I could taste his lower lip. His lashes fluttered shut as we indulged in a moment of lust that couldn't be put on hold any longer. "I think that can be arranged."

"I bought a ring, you know."

I pulled back so I could gape up at him. "You did? When?"

"Before I left to go rescue Lane. Mad's been holding onto it for me. I was going to work out this grand proposal, but you beat me to it. My proposal was a whole big thing that had Link singing in it, just so you know."

"Can I see the ring?" I asked, a small smile playing on my lips.

"Eventually. I still want my moment. Me down on one knee, you caught off-guard. I've got big plans for sweeping you off your feet."

"Consider me ready to be swept." I leaned up on my toes and brushed a kiss to his lips again.

He picked up my hand and eyed the finger with Kerdik's ring perched for the world to see. "It's not as nice as this one, but I think you'll like it."

"I love it already," I promised.

"It won't hold magic, but it'll keep me on your finger, there whenever you need me."

"I need you," I breathed, my arms snaking around his neck as his coiled around my hips. We slowly swayed to a beat all slow-dancers knew.

The rhythm soothed me, untying knots in my mind that had been too tightly bound. Only Bastien could relax me enough to gain such unequaled clarity. Hope shot through me, filling my lungs like helium expanding the skin of a balloon.

When I stopped our dance, Bastien studied my face with a look of concern. "Daisy? What is it?"

"I think I know how to get us to Morgan's castle." I looked down at my ring, wondering how I hadn't thought of it before now. "I can summon her."

"Summon who?"

"This ring has all of Faîte's lost magic in it. It's not just connected to Avalon; it's linked to Éireland too."

"So?"

"I don't think it's just Kerdik I can reach with this." A thrill of trepidation ran through my veins as I pressed the ring to my heart and whispered, "Cailleach, Cailleach, Cailleach."

7

THE BEAUTIFUL HAG

Bastien was none too pleased with me, and drew his knife in case... I don't know, but he seemed to think a knife would do the trick to get us out of whatever pickle I'd landed us in. "You'd better pray that didn't work. You have no idea what you're doing, summoning the hag."

I frowned at him. "That's kind of mean, don't you think? People can't help how they look."

"She calls herself 'the hag'. It's her title." He moved me back into a corner and stood in front of me, shielding my body from the empty room. Every muscle in his neck and arms were tensed, making me rethink the brilliance of the plan I'd not totally thought through.

A tinkling sound made my arm wrap around Bastien's middle. Chimes that sounded like Christmas bells and reminded me of Santa Claus echoed off the stone walls all around us. Beneath the beauty, I heard Bastien mutter a string of nervous swears. "Stay back, Rosie."

"She can't kill us," I reminded him, rubbing his stomach from behind.

Snow began to fall from the ceiling, adding a brisk temperature to the cozy room. The lamplight flickered in a one-two-three rhythm, matching my heartrate and warning me that I'd really stepped in it this time. The snow on the ceiling was localized in the center of the room, falling like a shower curtain and making a blind spot so thick, I couldn't tell what was going on behind it. When I heard the cackle that could rival any evil queen, my spine stiffened, and I held Bastien to me even tighter.

A woman's shrill voice sounded from behind the curtain of snow. "Who dares invoke such powerful magic tha could summon me all the way from Éireland?"

I couldn't see her, but answered the veil of winter all the same. "I did, your majesty. Rosie Avalon, a friend of Kerdik's."

Cailleach's voice scoffed in disbelief. "Kerdik has no friends."

"Kerdik has lots of friends. Bastien and I are only two of the people who care about him. He's in danger, and I didn't know who else to turn to."

"My dear green friend obviously didn't care to tell ye all he's done to my dear sister, Brìghde, or else ye wouldn't presume I'd lift a finger to help him."

I stepped out from behind Bastien, unwilling to cower from the meeting *I'd* called to order. I rolled my shoulders back, wondering when it was that I'd allowed my fear to call the shots. "Brìghde and Kerdik have been taken hostage. They had their magic stripped from them. They can't be killed, but they're stuck and they can't escape. You might not care about Kerdik, but I know you need Brìghde to balance Éireland."

Cailleach pfft'd from behind her curtain. "You're mistaken. My sister is just fine. I would know if she'd gone missing."

I put my hands on my hips. "You want to look out for Éireland all on your own? Because that's what we're dealing with here. Kerdik watches after Avalon by himself, and it's exhausting. Why, not too long ago he had to sleep to recharge his magic. Is that what you want?"

The silence that greeted me meant that I had earned a point on her. "Ye say Brìghde and Kerdik were taken together?"

I nodded, glad we were finally getting somewhere. "Brìghde took a mortal for a boyfriend, and he turned double agent on her. His name was Gilliam. He was working for Morgan le Fae, who used the secrets she confessed to him to manipulate your sister and steal her tears. Apparently there's some serious Jiu-Jitsu in there, because Morgan used them to cast a spell that weakened Kerdik and Brìghde."

The pause was telling, and though I'd been firm to the

point of antagonistic with her, she was beginning to let go of her distrust. "I told her no good could come from taking up with tha man. But no, no one listens to the hag."

"Well, you were right on this point, so high-five for you. He even lied to her about his real name. He lured her to Morgan's castle in Avalon, and now Morgan's captured her. She's burning Brìghde with some kind of acid that keeps her magic from restoring. She keeps shrieking in pain, and I know you don't want that for your sister."

The snow fell harder now, piling up and making a small hill. I shivered in my tank top, but knew I couldn't exactly put a winter-wielding sorceress on hold so I could fish around for a sweater.

"Morgan le Fae is truly hurting Brìghde?"

"And Kerdik. I want to go and help them both, but I can't get there."

"Ye want to use my magic so ye can free your friend."

"Yes, ma'am. My friend, a few members of my family, and your sister."

"I didn't know Brìghde had friends in Avalon. Ye want to rescue my sister? Ye must be close."

"She's never met me before. I don't know her, but I know Kerdik sacrificed himself to try and rescue her, which is how he got trapped there in the first place. If she's important to Kerdik, then she's important to me." I declared my allegiances with no room for debate.

All at once, the last layer of snow fell to the pile in a

gust, revealing a stooped old woman with a spindly cane. She had a missing tooth in front, a wonky left eye, pale and flaky skin, and blue dreads.

It wasn't the super cool blue dreadlocks that drew me to her, but the hump on her shoulders that tugged at my heart. "You... Your back."

"Yes?" Cailleach sneered, daring me to insult her.

"I look like you."

Cailleach clearly had not been expecting me to say this, since now we looked nothing alike. But I saw myself in her, the girl I used to be before Avalon found me.

I closed my eyes and shook my head, my childhood nickname coming back to haunt me. I loathed being called the Humpback Whale, and knew the damage such personal remarks made on a girl's psyche. "I was taken from Avalon when I was just a baby. My aunt stole me from my mother, Morgan le Fae, and took me to Common, where we hid until last year. My aunt had to change my appearance, and I think she used you as a guide. My eyes used to be the same as yours, pointing in two different directions." I reached over my shoulder to tap my back. "I had a hump, just like yours."

Cailleach eyed me bitterly. "Lies. You're fair – lovelier than most, actually – with no trace of any of those things."

I took a step forward, showing her my empty hands in innocence. My heart broke for her, living life unable to stand up straight. There was a certain power about possessing that ability now which I did not take for granted. "I see you," I told her, knowing the pain that came from being ostracized. Immortal and all-powerful or not, those were hard imperfections to live with. I'd only had just over two decades to suffer through, but she'd lived stooped like this forever.

I moved slowly forward so she could see I wasn't a threat. I could practically feel Bastien silently warning me to come back to him, but I didn't listen. I'm not sure he was surprised by that.

When I finally reached Cailleach, I warned her with a soft, yet stern look, that I was going to hug her, and she would deal with the gentle touch. I knew that kindness could feel threatening when you were used to cruelty. My arms slowly banded around her, and I even went so far as to lay my head on her stooped shoulder, offering myself as a refuge from the cold she seemed to travel with. She was my height, stooped as she was.

"Child, what are ye doing?" Her tone sounded a mix between irritable, touched and amused.

"This is a hug," I explained, knowing that of all the lifetimes of experience this woman had of seeing all the amazing things life offered up, Lane had given me the upper hand on this area of expertise. "Your hair is awesome, by the way. Mine's pretty boring."

Cailleach's body vibrated with a bemused chuckle, and finally her arm banded around my back, while her other hand remained clutching her cane. "You're lying to me. I can tell ye never had a hump, girl. But it was a sweet lie, so I'll forgive ye."

"I did," I promised. "You can ask my aunt. I was a sexy vixen with it, too. Rocked that hump like none other. My Aunt Lane changed my appearance to look more like you, I guess. She was worried my mother's army would find and capture me. The second her concealment charm wore off, she was right. Avalon found me, and now here I am." My voice quieted. "I know what it is to walk around stooped. I know how it feels when people look at you, then look away. I get it, and I think you're beautiful."

Cailleach kept vacillating from stiff to soft in my arms, unsure what the crap to do with me. My heart broke for the stares and pointing she'd no doubt endured far longer than I ever had to deal with it all. You had to build up a callous to get through life being the kind of person people couldn't look in the eye without wincing. I couldn't imagine how thick her skin would have to be to put up with it all for an eternity.

Cailleach cleared her throat. "Thank you, child."

When I stepped back, Cailleach's skin started to sparkle – the snow on her pale arms turning iridescent in the lantern's light. "Whoa, what..." I gasped when she stood straight, her hump suddenly fading away. I couldn't help the shriek that ripped from my mouth when her wrinkled skin began smoothing out, making her go from the age of seventy-five to maybe thirty-five. She scrutinized me with eyes that suddenly pointed in the same direction, going from "the hag" with super cool hair, to a gorgeous woman with super cool hair. "What just happened? How did you do that?" I balked, pointing to her form. "You just turned diva!"

Cailleach's slight intake of breath at my reaction made me wary, wondering if I'd crossed some line by commenting on her appearance. "What do you see, child?"

"You just knocked forty years off your age! Your hump is gone and your lazy eye is straight! How? Was it the same concealment charm that mutated me?"

Her expression went from cautious to emotional, the swing of it making Bastien take a step back. "Ye can see me? You've seen my true self?"

"Uh, care to explain that?"

Moisture welled in Cailleach's eyes, her gaze locking in on mine as if I was the first person to ever treat her like a human being (which, of course, she wasn't). "There was a spell cast on me long ago. I vexed Carman, so she cursed me."

"Who's Carman?"

"She's the first immortal, and wicked as they come. Now people see the hag when they meet me – the façade Carman covered me with. Only immortals and truly pure souls can see me as I really am." Her insecurity, her pain, and a little bit of triumph shone out in her expression. I saw the agony of isolation and the social stigma we all like to pretend we don't feel when we're ostracized. She reached out and gripped my hand as if she needed me, and not the other way around. "I haven't been seen in so very long. Only my sister and Kerdik know my true form. And now ye do, too."

8

CAILLEACH TURNING COLD

I went in for another hug, because when you go through a giant shift, it helps to have someone anchoring you to the planet. "I see you, and either way, I think you're super cool. You can hang with me anytime." When I stepped back, Bastien caught my eye with his wary and careful steps toward my side. "This is my fiancé, Bastien." I smiled at his stiff movements.

When he reached us, he knelt down, dipping his head in respect. "Your majesty."

Cailleach raised her eyebrow at me. "You've taken an Untouchable into your bed? How fitting. I see he's given ye his mark. Congratulations to ye both. I can see how even the strongest man might fall for your charms."

"Oh, it's all him. He gives me one of these," I paused to shimmy my shoulders, shaking my boobs a little just to make her laugh, "and I just can't help myself."

Cailleach chuckled. "I can imagine." Then she postured and rolled her shoulders back, getting down to business. "You say my Brìghde is being held by your mammy? How is this possible?"

I shook my head. "I'm not sure." I explained the vision I'd had through Kerdik's eyes, and the steps that led me to this moment of needing such a grand favor. "So I need to get there, but you can't port me into the castle. Otherwise, your magic might fade away, and Morgan might eventually find a way to snatch it up, like she's trying to do with Brìghde and Kerdik."

"I'm not afraid of a mortal, least of all a woman of Avalon. Your people aren't made of sturdy stuff, like mine are." She eyed me with confusion. "And what about your magic? Ye said Morgan le Fae has a way of detecting strong magic, which means you'd be a target, too."

My nose crinkled. "I don't have strong magic. I have my birth blessings, sure, but nothing more impressive than that."

Cailleach chuckled, as if I'd said something foolish. "Oh, wee princess. Those blessings are so strong, they no doubt transferred even up to your life in Common." Then she reached out her hand and grasped my fingers with an arthritic grip that belied the creamy, youthful hand. She stared intently into my eyes as she squeezed my fingers with a purposeful hint of a threat, holding me in place. "I see what Kerdik did, and it's only made your magic stronger. Brìghde told me he gave a mortal woman his blood, but I guess I had to see it to believe it."

I lowered my voice, though I knew no one could hear us. "That's not totally public information. Kerdik did that to save my life."

"Aye. Brìghde did tha for a mortal once before, and it ended in heartbreak. It's a grand thing for us to find someone we can give part of ourselves to. I'm surprised my green friend finally found someone he wants to keep around for two lifespans." She tilted her chin so she could look me in the eyes. "Are ye worthy?"

It was a question I knew the answer to without a blink. "No." Cailleach studied me while Bastien stiffened, but I didn't bother backpedaling.

Cailleach cackled at my response – actually cackled. "I like tha. Ye say ye want to rescue my Brìghde? I can help conceal your magic for a time. It won't work on an immortal, because we're too powerful to be stuffed away. But your abilities can be cloaked, strong as they are." She motioned for me to step back, and Bastien moved with me. "Step aside, boy."

Bastien shook his head. "With all due respect, I'm her *Guardien*, and her fiancé. Where she goes, I go."

Cailleach grinned at the pickle I'd landed myself in. "So Kerdik finally found someone he trusts, dare I say loves, and she's engaged to another man? A more fitting punishment I couldn't have thought up myself for tha manipulative cretin."

I narrowed my eyes at her. She'd called Kerdik her friend and a cretin in the span of half a minute. I wasn't totally sure how to read their relationship. "I know we don't know each other, but maybe our interactions could be less talk about running down one of my closest friends. Kerdik can be a good man; he just needs people to let him try."

"Is tha so? I know a very different side of him."

"I'm sure you do. But he's a prisoner right now, and if we don't set him free, then you'll have to deal with Avalon's whining along with Éireland's single-handedly. So if you're going to help us, I vote for now rather than later."

"You've got quite the noisy gob on ye."

I shrugged without pretense of apology.

Bastien held tight to my hand, and then coiled his arm around my hips, drawing me to his chest. "We'll do what we can to set Brìghde and Kerdik free, but be prepared to help Brìghde. She's pretty bad off right now. Morgan le Fae's been torturing her."

The stone walls surrounding us started to frost over and grow a layer of ice. I shivered, burrowing in Bastien's embrace while Cailleach started murmuring in a language I didn't know. My spine tingled with the chill, but it was equal parts the temperature, and the trepidation of not knowing what kind of help I might be getting from her.

"Bastien?" I eked out quietly, worried I might've done something stupid in summoning Cailleach. Maybe it wasn't my brightest idea, exposing us to magic we couldn't control, and had no say in. Kerdik was my safety net, and he wasn't here.

Bastien held me tight, his arms banding around my back to let me know that whatever destiny we were bound for, he was in it with me. "I've got you," he promised, though I could tell he was apprehensive.

Cailleach's murmuring picked up in volume, and then doubled until she was shouting at us. I gasped when her irises disappeared, turning her eyeballs completely white. The snow began to fall in thick clumps from the ceiling, stacking up all around us. The incantation sounded angry now, with syllables that sounded harsh and guttural.

I shrieked when the chill wasn't just a feeling, but became a touch that jerked at my body like chilled, slippery fingers that couldn't be trusted.

I was ripped from Bastien and thrown against the iced wall on the other side of the room, the wind knocked out of me. Hard and thick chunks of ice jutted out and coiled around my ankles and wrists, securing me to the wall while I screamed fruitlessly. Cailleach did the same to Bastien, banding ice around his legs, torso and arms so we were separated, and could do nothing but stare in fear at each other as we shouted and struggled with our bindings.

Cailleach used her tall, spindly cane to inch her way toward me. She eyed my finger, which was powerless to do more than ball into a fist to resist her. She pried open my hand, studying my ring with a hard look to her, now that her irises had returned. "Ye summoned me," she observed.

"Kerdik's in trouble! You have to let me go! I'm the only one who can kill Morgan and stop this whole thing!" My ankles were painful with the hardness of the ice, and the arctic nature of my bindings. Still, I struggled for all I was worth.

When Cailleach twirled the ring around on my finger, I panicked. "Stop! The last person who tried to take off my ring died! Kerdik put a spell on it that only he could take it off me."

Cailleach studied my face for lies, but that's the thing about the truth being stranger than fiction. She leaned in and sniffed my ring, rubbing her wet nose against my knuckles. "You're not lying. Kerdik really did think of everything. I wonder what he's hiding in your ring. How did ye summon me?" She straightened, so she could look me in the eye. "Kerdik caused Brìghde no small amount of heartache, using her as he did. He ended her marriage, after she'd given her husband a double portion of life, as ye have. Tha Kerdik's got his sights set on ye makes ye very intriguing to me. I'll help ye rescue my Brìghde, wee princess, but after tha, you'll explain to me how it was ye found a way to summon me. Not even my most faithful servants can do tha."

I shivered, just wanting the whole thing to be over. "Kerdik gave me abilities I don't totally understand. He doesn't talk to me about them; he just does his thing and doesn't feel the need to explain himself."

"Ah, now tha does sound like Kerdik. Had ye said

anything else, I don't think I'd have believed it." She tapped the ring twice, and then stepped back. "Your ring knows me."

I spoke through chattering teeth. "Dude, I've g-g-got no idea what that means."

Only I *did* know. Éireland's lost magic was hidden inside my ring. Though it was in plain view of Cailleach, no one assumed Kerdik would entrust me with such a dangerous trinket.

Cailleach closed the gap between us, sizing me up for who knows what purpose. I tried to hold my chin high and keep my composure, but when her cane bumped to the ring on my right hand, heat shot through both of us. I screamed, and Cailleach dropped her cane, jumping back as if the twisted wood had bitten her. "What did ye do?" she accused me with wide eyes.

"Nothing! What could I p-p-possibly do, frozen to the wall like this? Your cane burned me!" It scared me that something had happened that not even an immortal could explain away. Her look of alarm matched my own.

Cailleach lifted up her cane with caution, checking it for cracks. Then she looked at me with wide eyes, as if I was the danger, though I hadn't done a thing.

Bastien called out for me, angry as he struggled fruitlessly against his bindings. "Let her go! If you're not going to help us, then let Rosie go."

Cailleach reached out and squeezed my chin, smooshing my cheeks in that way old ladies did that made you feel like a five-year-old, no matter how grown you got. She studied my mismatched irises with a careful eye. "Why did Kerdik give ye his blood?"

I swallowed hard. "To heal m-m-me when I was almost d-d-dead."

"He's in love with ye, then." She jerked her chin in the direction of the end table, which still held the stone vase he'd made me, along with the yellow roses that never lost an ounce of their luster. "Those are from him. I can tell his signature. He put them there so he could find ye, and ward off anyone who might come looking for trouble."

I closed my eyes through a shiver that rocked my body. The ice at my back was freezing through my tank top, setting a cold deep down in my spine. "I d-d-don't want to t-t-talk about it."

"Don't think tha just because I'm granting ye my help this one time, I'll be persuaded to lift his curse." She wrenched my jaw in her deceptively strong grip and jerked her head in Bastien's direction. "The day ye throw this brute aside and go for Kerdik is the day Avalon gets another dragon."

"Dude, stop evil villain monologuing, and help us get them out of there! I'm past my patience with people in power threatening me. Either help us or don't!"

Cailleach stepped back, dropping her hand from my face in surprise that I had the gall to talk back to her. "Very well." She waved her cane toward my bed, said, *"cacher la magie,"* and out from the tip of her cane shot a puff of snow that feathered over my mattress. When she blew away the flakes, two black capes were lying there. "Wear those, and it'll conceal most of the magic you're carrying. Kerdik's blood in ye will be detected if ye step outside of that cape. Be sure ye stay tight inside of it. If your Untouchable wears his, you'll be able to see each other, but no one will be able to see either of ye." Then she clicked her fingers, and just like that, the ice fell away from us, loosening our limbs so we both collapsed to our knees. I wanted to crawl to Bastien, but my limbs were immobile from the freeze. My whole body felt like one giant icicle that might break if it was moved.

Cailleach rolled her eyes at us, as if our inability to move was our own fault, and not hers. She moved slowly to the capes, lifting them and then draping them over our shoulders. I gasped when Bastien disappeared, but then reappeared when my own cape was donned. It was like walkie-talkies, but for sight.

Bastien was the first to be able to move, and he stumbled toward me with all the ferocious determination of the warrior I knew he was. "I've g-g-got you," he promised again, wrapping his icy arm around my back, so we could freeze together in our misery.

I huddled into him, afraid that I'd once again bitten off more than I could chew. Still, Bastien didn't desert me, but offered his freezing body up as my shelter, tucking me in the safety of his arms and shielding my body with his. Not once did he remind me that this was all on me, since I'd summoned Cailleach. I adored him for being a man who loved me more than he clung to being right.

His words had venom in them when he finally was steady enough to speak to her. "You take your anger out on me, n-n-not her." Then he gave her the coordinates of the castle.

Cailleach looked down her upturned nose at Bastien. "I'll do as I please. Now, see tha ye don't disappoint in bringing my Brìghde home. I'll not always be as pleasant as I was today." With a boom that seemed to shake the castle, Cailleach and my walled-in bedroom disappeared from our view.

My eyes jerked shut as the world went dark and seemed to suck at our skin. I opened them two seconds later, when our bodies were slammed into the grass at the back of my mother's property. Cailleach was nowhere to be found in the twilight, instead leaving us to our shock and unrelenting shivers.

9

VEGETARIAN WITH A KNIFE

For several long minutes, neither of us stood, but chose to huddle together like children who'd escaped a natural disaster. "I'm s-s-sorry, Bastien. I didn't know she'd hate Kerdik so much."

Bastien kept the lecture stapled tight inside of him. "There's nothing for it now. Let's get ourselves together and make a plan." His arms around me were unbending, capturing me in his love. The tight compression calmed my shivering as the warmth of Avalon slowly trickled into my pores, unlocking my stiff body. When I finally slumped in his arms, he somehow found the strength to hold me together. "Hey," he whispered when he felt me despairing. "It's going to be alright. You got us here. It was risky, but it worked. I say we get Lane and them out first, since Kerdik and Brìghde might be more difficult to bust free."

I nodded, brushing my cheek against his hard, flannelled chest. "You know I love you, right?"

"I have a very short memory about that, so you might have to remind me every day for the rest of our lives." His frosty fingers found my face, fingering my jaw as if I was something delicate and precious. "I don't like anyone laying a hand on my wife. From the first time I met you, there was this draw to make sure no one ever hurt you. Then I ended up doing most of the hurting." He moved his cheek to mine, so we could share a little body heat. "Then when I took your *lueur*, that pull you had on me grew until it was unbearable to be apart. Now that you're going to be my wife?" He steadied his grip on me, communicating with the tight hold how scared he'd been. "I can't handle seeing you in pain. It breaks me up inside. I can see myself throwing people out of the way and moving whole buildings just to make sure you're alright."

My lips found his and offered up a quaking kiss. "I'm alright. No more injured from the cold than you are."

Bastien couldn't stop touching my face, so I let him, since it seemed to calm him down from the fear that we'd almost been torn apart by an immortal. "When we get in there, you have to direct us, but I want you to stay behind me. If something comes for us, you get hit last. Understood?"

I wanted to argue, but knew there was no point. "You can lead for now, since you have the knives."

He let out a nervous bluster of a chuckle. "That looked like it was hard for you to say. Well done."

My gut tugged me toward the castle, so I stood on shaking legs, tying my cape around my neck with stiff fingers. The hood went over my head, and though there were half a dozen soldiers in the distance, they didn't give any indication that they'd seen me. I smirked at Bastien when he fiddled with the ties on his cape. "You're pretty in that thing," I commented with a light kiss to his lips.

"I want you to remember that you called me pretty. You might forget, after I start laying out the soldiers who messed with Reyn."

"Will do, princess."

"Hmm." He squinted at me, and then picked up my hand to move it to his belt under his cape, so that we moved together towards the castle.

I shuddered when my gaze fell to the well near where we were at the back of the property. The dark that was quickly falling around us spooked me as I recalled the narrow tunnel I had been dropped in. I closed my eyes against Bastien when he drew me to his side so we walked in-step. My mother had dumped me down a well over a piece of jewelry. Ain't no shrink qualified to wade through that sewage without a hazmat suit. "Bastien?"

"Yeah, babe?" His gaze was on the soldiers we were stalking as we neared the castle.

"Don't let Morgan throw me down that well."

Bastien stopped suddenly and turned so I could see his

serious expression. "After today, I won't let anyone put their hands on you ever again. I'll take you somewhere safe, and we'll have a life where you don't have to look at this awful place ever again."

I leaned up on my toes to kiss him before we kept moving. I didn't like feeling defenseless, but that's exactly what you are when you're at the bottom of a well. Bastien loved me when I was strong, charging into a guarded castle armed with only a couple knives. He also loved me when I was weak, emaciated, and couldn't lift my head to greet him. That's a good man, and I knew how lucky I was to have him by my side.

"Stay back," Bastien warned.

When we neared the soldiers, Bastien handed me one of his shorter knives, and drew a third from his boot. Because, why wouldn't he have an arsenal in his wardrobe? He motioned to the two men on the right, deciding to end them before he finished off the two on the left. There were three others, but they were farther away, and would be dealt with next.

It felt like cheating when I stabbed one of the soldiers in the side of his neck. I tried not to make a sound, but my panic at the dark deeds I was doing welled up in my throat like too much vomit. Though I'd helped Bastien kill Armand and Silvain in the beginning of our journey together, it never got any easier.

My second victim fell with only a tiny squeak that I let out when I drove my knife through his abdomen, letting him fall to the grass as he cried out he'd been attacked. My hand went over his mouth as the other two men bounded for the dying. Bastien's kills were cleaner and quicker than mine as he intercepted them, but whatever. I blamed my clumsy cuts on me being a vegetarian.

When the remaining three in the distance responded to the slight noises of disturbance, Bastien was ready. The trio descended on their fallen brethren, but Bastien ended them without so much as a grunt, his knife flashing in the rising moonlight.

He frowned with frustration up at me as he grabbed one of the bodies under the armpits. "I told you I would handle it, and for you to stay back. Something confusing about that?"

I shook my head, trying to appear contrite. "Seven on one didn't seem fair. I don't like the thought of people fighting you."

"Well, I don't like the thought of blood on your hands." He hefted the body to the castle wall, and then reached for another. "I also don't like you in a lifeless pile on the ground!"

"I'll try my best not to get stabbed, then."

Bastien mimed laughing at my lame attempt at humor as we pulled the bodies to rest against the stone wall of the castle, so they wouldn't be super visible. He affixed my hand to his belt again and coiled his arm around my back, so we walked together into the castle, and toward our family.

10

———

MY FRIEND AND MY ENEMY

I could've closed my eyes and still found our way, but they were wide as saucers, confused as I took in the castle that was dimly lit by the occasional candle. Though it had never seemed cheery to me, now it felt downright grim. The walls weren't as clean, the stone shining with a layer of grayish grime. It smelled like mildew everywhere, and nowhere did the familiar scent of Fabien, the cook's, freshly baked bread or delicious soups reach my senses.

We moved on stealthy feet through the stone corridors, since Cailleach hadn't explained whether or not our sounds were being concealed. I stopped a few times and turned us in a different direction, since my gut was harder to feel when I was nervous. I wanted to tell Bastien that maybe he should wait outside so he didn't get hurt, but talking wasn't really a thing you could do in stealth-mode.

The few people we passed didn't take notice of us, though my heart pounded loudly all the same. Most were household servants, keeping their heads down as they walked in their sandals through the castle. We were almost to the point my gut was tugging me toward when a familiar voice stopped me in my tracks. My gasp stayed tucked inside of me as Bastien and I flattened our backs to the dirty wall. It had never been dirty when I'd lived here. I frowned at the oversight that meant the man coming toward me was dropping the ball.

"See that the prisoners are fed and watered again," Rigby said to the man he was walking with, pausing just a few feet from where we stood.

"But her majesty most high said no more than once a day."

Rigby's voice was firm with the command he held over the household. "Then see it's done quietly, and tell the prisoners to eat and drink quickly. I'll not have the Lost Duchess die in a dungeon. The rest of Avalon would have our heads."

"You're going soft, Master Rigby," the young man commented, his shoulder-length black hair falling into his face.

Rigby's tone turned sharp, though he did not besmirch his graceful demeanor by raising his voice. "I'll assign you to warm Morgan le Fae's bed tonight, if you keep up that kind of talk."

"No, Master Rigby! I wasn't saying anything bad against you. I only meant that you're..."

"I know what you meant. Perhaps a week in her majesty most high's bed will teach you the value of kindness in such a cruel world."

The young man lowered his shoulders, his chin dipping to the ground. "Yes, Master Rigby. I'll see to the prisoners, and keep it quiet from the staff and her majesty most high."

"Very good. On your way, now." When the man left, Rigby remained in the hallway, pausing as if in thought. He inhaled deeply and closed his eyes, then whipped his head around in confusion. "Princess?"

I stiffened against the wall, amazed that Rigby was so details-oriented that he could pick me out by the scent of my skin. Bastien gripped my hand, unnecessarily warning me not to make our presence known.

Rigby inhaled again, though this time it looked as though the memory of me pained him. He pressed his hand over his heart and he closed his eyes, bathing in the slight fragrance of my skin. "Forgive me," he whispered, almost like a prayer, as if the mere smell of flowers cut through the toughened exterior of his soul.

It was difficult to be so near to him. I didn't know what I would've said, had I the option of conversing right now. Part of me wanted to punch him, while another side of me wanted to rant and tear him a new one, sobbing while I recounted each moment in the well, where he'd left me to rot. I wanted to scream Demi's name in his face, demanding justice for my boyfriend, who hadn't been given a shred of grace in his shortened life.

The other part of me wanted to fall into his arms, as I had in my father's holding room when Urien had still been frozen in his slumber. Rigby let his guard down that day, assuring me that I had a friend in this cold, lonely place. My heart was too broken to be near him, and yet there he was, shattering my fragile pieces all over again by just looking at his pained expression.

Rigby's hand reached out so he could brace himself on the wall mere inches from my head. I was afraid to breathe, too scared to even blink. Though he was still proper in his fitted beige pants to match the white dress shirt underneath his standard red jacket with gold threading, I noticed the wavy brown hair that curled up at the base of his neck was slightly mussed. I wondered just what misfortune might result in Rigby presenting himself to the household in any way other than the height of composure, perfectly groomed.

I rallied everything in me, willing myself to one day forgive Rigby for the blind obedience that had landed me in the bottom of a well. He'd seen me mostly naked, and I felt exposed in his presence. I counted the seconds through his steady inhales that seemed to invoke some sort of catharsis. The space between Rigby's eyebrows wrinkled, his eyes shut tight through pain that looked both physical and emotional.

I would have held him through that pain. I would have stayed up all night listening to every ounce of it.

But here we were – him in pain, and me afraid to breathe in his presence.

Bastien's hand moved to clutch his knife, but I put my palm atop his wrist to let him know that killing Rigby might not be the best move right now. Morgan relied on him for everything. If we wanted time to get everyone out before we went after her, Rigby needed to be kept in the dark, and the house needed to be business as usual.

Plus, I'm not sure my heart could take the sight of him bleeding out on the stone floor. Angry as I was, I was too conflicted about it all to wish him dead.

After a few more beats, Rigby collected himself and moved down the hall. Bastien and I didn't move until the footsteps had long faded. Seeing Rigby left me shaken, so when I reached out for Bastien this time, it wasn't purely just so we could stay together through the maze. I wanted him close so I didn't feel naked, exposed in front of a man whom I'd thought was my friend, until it turned out I was wrong.

I didn't like being wrong about that. I liked to believe the best in people. But Rigby tricked me, hurt me, and left me for dead. I didn't like to think about that whole mess, but seeing him invoked a fear in me I couldn't reconcile. I felt sad for the state of the world, that there were duplicitous people who could do such unthinkable things.

He'd duped me into believing he was my friend – that he was a good guy. I was the dummy who fell for his beautiful lies that I wasn't alone, and that he would be there for me.

Rigby had known all along that I was stupid.

11

DOWN TO DEPTHS WITH THE DAMNED

Bastien's arm around me tightened, sensing my despair, but keeping quiet through the worst of it.

I checked in with my gut and led us down a set of stone steps I'd never investigated before. The mildew stench grew as the corridor seemed to narrow. Instead of only black and gray grime on the walls, now there were streaks of red. Smeared bloody handprints from prisoners fighting for their freedom screamed at us, letting us know we were visiting the damned.

My gut was tugging at me with all its might when we reached a solid wooden door at the bottom of the stone steps. Bastien gently pushed against it, but the door didn't budge. "Locked," he whispered with a tight frown. I could hear groaning and the clinking of chains on the other side, but I couldn't get to the prisoners. I pressed my palm to the door and closed my eyes, willing Lane to feel that I was near, and for that hope to give her peace through her fear. I gulped with dread when it dawned on me that some of those bloody handprints might've been hers.

Taking a deep breath, I checked in with my gut for the key. My inner guide told me to stand against the wall. I did as my Compass instructed, yanking Bastien to my side to obey. He didn't say a word, but trusted me to get the job done.

We waited in complete silence for seven minutes, letting the groans and intermittent wails of the prisoners fill our ears. Bastien was ready to attack – I could feel his muscles tensing with the frustration of being stuck on the wrong side of the door.

When heavy boots descended the stairs behind the unsteady shuffle of a no doubt weary prisoner, we sucked in our stomachs to give them ample room in the tight space. The warden was swinging a lantern, which shed just enough light to ensure neither of them tripped and smooshed us. I couldn't help the gasp when I saw none other than Duke Henri being brought down before the stoic guard. My uncle was stooped now, unable to stand straight as he hobbled like a troll. He had a freshly bleeding lower lip, a long cut on his temple, and a limp that bespoke a busted hip.

The guard didn't seem to derive pleasure from controlling every step of the once powerful ruler, but simply did his job – punching the clock without a thought. His forward eyes didn't sweep to us, nor did he seem to care that his red vest with gold trim was stained with dried blood and grime.

Bastien reached out and caught the lip of the door before it shut, swinging it open just enough for us to both slip through. The door shut behind us, but we didn't move from it. Instead, we took in the scene with mouths agape.

Prisoners were kept in the dark that was now only lit by the stoic warden's swinging lantern. They were in separate cells that stood no more than four feet tall by four feet wide. They couldn't stand, and couldn't stretch out on the floor.

"Not the cage! I won't go back in there!" Uncle Henri roared, suddenly coming out of his stupor. He turned and moved his stiff fists to try his hand at combat, but the guard only rolled his eyes.

"You know your time in the sun is over, old man." The warden popped Duke Henri in the jaw, sending him stumbling back in a stupor. The open cage was behind him, and the guard kicked Uncle Henri in his bum hip, not bothering to catch him when Henri fell on the hard stone. The warden sighed, as if to say, "This is the lamest job in the world. When's my fifteen?" He shoved Henri into the cage and locked it with the key on his belt.

"Why?" Henri groaned.

"Because her majesty most high absorbed your province. You yourself signed the papers that she could do what best suited Province 1's needs. Having only one ruler is what does that." He shook his head. "I'd be mad at you for giving up such a strong region if it wasn't so sad. That you thought she'd let you sit on the throne by her side? Rich people don't pay attention to shit." He scoffed at the stupidity, and I really couldn't blame the guy. Henri had been dumb to think Morgan would be cool sharing power. She only ever took from those around her.

"Leave him alone," came a voice that made my heart ache. "Don't touch my father!"

I wanted to call out to Draper, to let him know that help was here, and to shut up so he didn't catch himself a beating, but I knew I couldn't make myself known yet.

The guard kicked the cage next to Henri's, the flickering lamplight falling on my sweet brother. He was missing his shirt, and had crusty cuts all over his back. It looked like someone had taken a whip to him. I knew I couldn't compromise my vision with bloody tears, so I kept my grief locked in my heart. I bit down on my lower lip to keep from shouting all the things that were wrong with the state of the world.

"Do you need to put in more time at the whipping post?" The guard didn't seem pissed at Draper's outburst, but more annoyed.

"Quiet, honey," Lane cooed from the cell on the other side of Draper's. "My son didn't mean anything by it. He doesn't need to be whipped again. I can keep him quiet."

"See that you do." The guard squatted down to peer into Lane's cage, casting light on her dirty face and haunted eyes. "I don't like keeping you down here, Duchess, but I'm a good soldier who follows commands."

Lane nodded with sadness pulling at her usually perky smile. "I understand. We'll be good. Please don't hurt my boy anymore."

"You don't have to stick up for me, Lane. I can handle the whipping post," Draper seethed.

Her voice turned sharp with emotion. "Well, I can't! Do you think your scars only hurt you? They break me!"

The guard didn't acknowledge Draper, but addressed only Lane. "I won't mess him up if he can keep his outbursts to himself. I don't get off on beating prisoners who haven't done a thing wrong to Avalon. You all give me a quiet night with no fuss, and I'll leave you all alone. Sound good?"

"Sounds good. Thank you, Astin."

Lane could charm even the most hardened soldier. Who knows how many prisoners he'd had to torture like this, yet Lane had found a way to soften him back into a malleable human. That was the magic of a good mom.

It was too much to expect me to stay dormant against the wall when Lane was in a cage. Bastien put his finger to his lips to warn me he would get the key. He wore a sneer of barely contained fury when his eyes fell on the cell on the other side of Lane. The steel prison held Reyn's figure, which was shrouded in shadow. Reyn wasn't moving, but was a pile of limbs on the stone floor. Bastien's boots were soundless as he crept up on the warden, but he began to lose his temper the closer he got to his target.

Bastien hefted Astin up and slammed him atop Duke Henri's cage, spittle flying out in barely contained rage. His words came out forced through gritted teeth that told me when the final blow came, it would be bloody, and without regret. "You put my mother in a cage," he growled, making my heart swoon that he could claim Lane as his own. When we got married, she would be his mother. I hadn't put that together until just now, but it seemed Bastien had been mulling over the specifics enough to attach himself to my family. He held his knife to Astin's throat. "You locked my brothers up like dogs."

Astin trembled with confusion, and though he was a big enough man, not being able to see your assailant could dishevel even the strongest soldier. "Who are you?" Astin worked out as he struggled fruitlessly against my beastly fiancé.

"Wrong question. You should be asking yourself who you are, to be locking a duchess in a cage. She's the beacon of the free world, and you're keeping her in the dark so the rest of the world goes blind. Have you been starving my mother?"

"No! I feed them more than her majesty most high allows."

"Have you laid a hand on my mother?"

"Of course he did!" Draper shouted, calling for revenge.

Astin scrambled for an answer. "I only ordered the beatings that are standard for all prisoners I oversee. You act like I have a choice in anything! You act like Morgan le Fae doesn't see all and control all!"

"Bastien, wait! He's only doing what he's told," Lane offered, gripping the bars on her cage with renewed hope. Like a good mother, she recognized his voice.

Bastien's knife was quick when it finally moved. The serrated edge swept across Astin's throat, spilling out red that dripped into Duke Henri's cage, painting him with crimson splashes. Bastien held Astin there while he choked and bled out, pinning him with one hand while he unhooked the key from Astin's belt. "I was in the army once too, and I chose to risk death because I knew what I was being ordered to do wasn't right. You always have a choice, and you chose wrong, Soldier. Choosing nothing is how the world starts crumbling." He leaned in, his volume controlled, but his voice shaking with rage. "I wanted more for Avalon than this! A true soldier fights harder for Avalon than he does his own life."

12

DUKE HENRI'S CHILDREN

"**G**et him off my cage!" Uncle Henri ordered. "Get us out quickly, before anyone else comes down here."

Bastien called to me over his shoulder. "Babe, could you grab the key?"

I ran forward as Lane moaned, "You didn't bring my daughter into this mess! Tell me you're not this reckless!" She looked around, unable to see either of us.

"Of course he didn't," I said quietly, swallowing the bile in my throat that rose at the sight of my mommy in a cage. "I'm back at your place right now, kicking my feet up and inventing new raps about ice cream with Judah."

I unlocked the door and gently pulled her out, careful with her stiff limbs. "Rosie," she cooed. "I never want to see my baby in a dungeon. Not that I can see you now, but still. How are you invisible?"

I draped the lip of my cape around her shoulders, letting her see my face. I tried to look confident, to assure her with my serenity that everything would be fine. "'I get by with a little help from my friends.'"

Bastien grumbled to Lane, "If you think I'm reckless, you should aim that lecture at your daughter. I don't have it in me to explain how we came across these cloaks. We'll save that story for when you can yell nice and loud. For now, let's get you out of here." Bastien sighed his frustration that Astin was taking more than five seconds to die. "Come on, already." Then, remembering himself, he started murmuring the soldier's prayer I'd heard him utter many times before. Despite the gore of the moment, it was sweet, and I respected him for the solid gesture.

I kissed Lane's cheek and moved to Draper's cage, unlocking him and guiding him out. He was so grateful to be out, he tackled me backwards, wrapping his arms around me as I giggled through the tame wrestle. He kissed my cheeks as tears fell from his eyes and dotted my face. "You have no idea, Rosie. I was sure we'd be lost down here forever! How'd you get here so quickly? Does the kingdom know we're being held captive?"

I tried to find the best way to hold him, but his back was so sliced up, it was hard to assure him of my affections. I settled for sitting next to him on the floor and combing my fingers through his matted and greasy hair. I brushed it away from his face so he looked more like a person again. His angular features had an edge of anger to them I'd not seen much of before. "Hey, it's alright. You're out now. No one's going to hurt you if I'm around."

Draper buried his nose in my cheek and chuckled, shifting on the floor with a grunt. I covered him with my cape, hugging his neck as he pulled me onto his lap. I felt small in Draper's arms, and like it was okay that I didn't have all the answers. We had each other, and somehow, that would be enough. "You shouldn't have come."

"They shouldn't have locked my brother in a cage. Don't you know I'll always rescue you?"

"Maybe I should know that by now, but you still constantly surprise me. Is our army outside? Are they ready to take us home? Where's Morgan's head being posted?"

I kissed his cheek and crawled off his lap over to Reyn's cage. "She's still alive. There's no cavalry, only Bastien and me." When the key unlocked his door, I was hoping that might rouse him. He didn't move, though. "Um, Lane? What happened to Reyn?"

Lane's voice was quiet and respectful. "He's been to the whipping post twice. He's alive, but he passed out from all the blood loss. Here, I'll help you with him." I shook my head at her and motioned for Bastien to leave his conquest and help me with the living. "You sit tight. Bastien and I will get him out."

Bastien let out quiet noises of distress when we finally worked Reyn out of the cage. His dark skin had been torn open in too many places, and he was cold to the touch.

"He's breathing," I ruled with relief. "We've got to get you guys out of here, but I don't know how. We offed the soldiers surveying the grounds behind the castle, but it's only a matter of time until they're found. I'm sure there are others making rounds, too."

"What happened to Kerdik?" Lane asked. "He ported us here, but as soon as we stepped into the castle, a gong sounded through the house and a whole mess of guards were on us in a second. He punched Morgan, and for no reason that I could see, he passed clean out. Is something wrong with him? Is that why he hasn't come for us?"

"Kerdik's in trouble, and we don't have much time." I looked up at Bastien. "Reyn's in no position to make a dash through the night. None of them are. What should we do?"

"Let me out!" Henri shouted, rattling the bars on his cage as droplets of blood sloped over his long nose. Astin was still bleeding all over him, painting his arms and shoulder-length greasy hair in a macabre crimson.

Bastien moved to the cage and kicked it just to spook Henri before he slid a short sword, a knife, a set of hand-cuffs and a whole ring of keys from Astin's dead body, pocketing them for his own use. "You'll stay put, for the good of all of Avalon." Then Bastien squatted down so he could look Duke Henri in the eye. "We were on the council together. I trusted you to look out for what was best for Avalon. You sold Province 2 to Morgan? What's more, you tried to marry your own niece when you knew I loved her."

Uncle Henri seethed like an animal, spittle and blood

dripping from his chin. "You will let me out of here so I can call my people home!"

Bastien paused to study Duke Henri's face. "No. You'll stay here, where you can't cause any further damage to Avalon."

Draper stiffened, but he didn't say anything to contradict Bastien's ruling.

"Let me out!"

Bastien was calm as he laid out Duke Henri's gravest sin. "You sided with the woman who captured Damond. You didn't care to track down your own son's ashes after he was burned by Morgan's soldiers!"

"I have no sons!" Henri rasped with fury over a life he no doubt wished he'd lived better.

Bastien looked around at the empty cages. "Where's your daughter? Gwen, I'll set free. It's the one kindness I'll grant you after all you put your people and us through.

"You'll leave me down here to die?"

Bastien was firm. "I'll not slit your throat in front of your son. Prison's the best place for a man who deserts the people who counted on him to protect them. I won't make Draper watch his father die."

Henri snarled in Draper's direction. "He's not my son."

Draper merely shrugged, his jaw tightening through the pain he was well-versed in compartmentalizing. I knelt next to my brother, claiming him when Province 2 in all of its foolishness would not.

Lane was livid, her temper mirroring my own. "That's right, he's not yours anymore; Draper's *my* son!"

Fury rose up in me, so I gripped Draper's hand to hold myself in place. He jerked, since he couldn't see me, but he calmed at the sound of my voice. "You're my brother. You belong to Lane and me now. No one will ever disown you like that again." Though I didn't want to leave my uncle in the cage, I knew he'd be a danger to us if he was released. "Let's go."

Lane wrapped her arms around Reyn on the floor, and motioned to the wall behind her. "Draper, show Bastien where Astin was keeping the extra weapons."

Draper tried to stand, but his back was bowed still. He was on all fours, as if he was still inside the cage. "Oh, honey!" I cooed, moving to his side and rubbing his shoulders.

"I'm alright. It's just been awhile since I've been upright. Oh, that feels good. Watch out for the cuts on my back, though. When you massage my shoulders, it's stretching some of the whip marks. I don't want to start bleeding again." He sat back on his heels, ignoring his father while Henri and Bastien argued and cussed at each other. "My arms. Start there, if you can."

"Of course." I massaged his forearms, working my way up to his biceps, and finally the meat of his shoulder. My hands moved gentler this time so I didn't rip open his cuts.

"Here. This won't feel great on your back, but it'll warm

you up." Bastien took off his flannel under his cape, sparing one of his two tops for my brother.

"Thanks, Bastien. To the left is a latch on the wall. If you tug on it, a few of the stones swing out. That's where the rest of the weapons are."

"On it." I worked on Draper, moving to his lower back when he laid down on the stone floor; it was a safer way of stretching out his unyielding muscles without toppling over. I straddled his butt and massaged the backs of his legs, working my way down until finally his legs laid flat on the stone.

I felt Henri's eyes on me, but didn't look up. "You're a disgrace, you know. Morgan le Fae's daughter, stroking her cousin's legs in a dungeon."

"Shut up," Draper groaned into the floor.

"Actually, it's way grosser than that, because Draper's not my cousin anymore; he's my brother. So we're super way disgusting." I rubbed Draper's ankles with gentle, steady pressure, rotating them first to the left and then to the right, so they could at least bend correctly when Draper tried to put weight on them. "The thing about me, though, is I'm on the other side of this cage. Insult me all you want, Bastien's not going to end it quick for you just because you try to piss us all off."

"You're an insolent brat! You got your mother's looks, but none of her grace."

"Aw, shucks. You know, I was thinking of moving into your old castle, now that you're not using it. I might just bring Draper back to live there, too. One big, happy family. Might even sit on your throne if I run out of extra chairs around the old dinner table. Where'd Gwen end up? Maybe I should invite her to throw darts at your portrait. Something tells me she might have a few daddy issues in need of venting."

Henri's chin quivered. "My daughter was going to make something of herself. Draper and Damond had too much of their mother in them. Weak."

I looked over my shoulder at Draper, whose eyes looked haunted. "'Was?' Is Gwen dead?"

"She was to visit Duchess Avril in Province 8. Gwen was going to offer an olive branch of peace to see if our provinces could join forces." Henri's voice shook with genuine sorrow. "I didn't expect her to receive such a harsh welcoming from Avril. The Duchess thought Gwen was there to steal her jewel, so she sent me back my daughter's head in a box. An old, dirty box." He paused for the memory that visibly haunted him, drawing out the hollows under his eyes. "That's when I knew I had to ally my land more securely with Morgan's."

Lane was fuming as she held Reyn on the grimy stone floor. "You sent your daughter to the woman who you know stole my jewel, Roland's and a third. You knew what evil was in Avril, but you sent Gwen there anyway. You didn't protect your daughter." She sneered at Henri in disgust. "Throw away the key," Lane directed to Bastien.

Bastien held the key in the material of the cape, so he

didn't burn himself as he lit the tip of the metal with the flame from the lantern. He heated it until the jagged shape started to melt. "Not a problem, Mom."

Lane managed a soft smile for Bastien. "Thank you, Son."

Henri howled his fury, but Bastien didn't stop until the job was done, and Duke Henri's freedom sufficiently destroyed.

13

———

THE BEST FRIEND A SPICE GIRL COULD
ASK FOR

It took some time, but eventually Lane and Draper were on their feet, and Reyn was conscious. Granted, he wasn't much more than barely awake, but I wasn't about to complain. Reyn leaned heavily on me and Draper, while Lane and Bastien debated what to do next. "This is taking too long, guys! Kerdik and Brìghde are being tortured. We have to get them out now!"

"We will, babe, but we can't get ourselves locked back up in the process. We have to get Reyn out of here first."

"I'll be fine," Reyn protested, though no one bothered to argue with his faulty assumption. Reyn was bad off, the whip marks still wet to the touch. He was shaky on his feet, but insisted Bastien would not carry him and damage what was left of his pride. "I vote we stay here."

"What?" Lane frowned at her fiancé. "Hun, we need to get out of here." Of the three of them, Lane had been quickest to be back on her feet, ready for action. Turns out she'd been let out of her cage most often, because Astin wanted to eat his meals with a legit duchess.

"How? None of us can make the trek with no provisions, beaten up as we are. Bastien should go and see if he can free Kerdik. Then Kerdik can get us out. All we have to do is defend the dungeon, which won't see a new guard for at least a few hours."

It was a terrible plan, but the only one we had to go on. Bastien and Lane were whispering conspiratorially while I tried to steady Reyn. Draper and I lowered him to the floor just to be sure he didn't collapse. Draper was doing a bit better now, but I wanted to get him out of here. "We'll be quick," I offered, though we all knew I had no control over how long it might take to overthrow a kingdom.

Lane pulled Draper to the side and spoke quietly to him, while Bastien wrapped Reyn's trembling fingers around a knife. "Stay strong, brother. I'll be back for you soon."

Reyn leaned forward and gripped Bastien's shoulder, bringing him down to rest his forehead against his friend's. They'd seen each other through so much; I hoped one day soon they'd be able to watch each other get married, and be the blissful family who lived happily ever after. "Don't be reckless, brother," Reyn begged. "It matters if you live."

Bastien smirked at Reyn, no doubt sharing several unspoken memories that only the best of friends could communicate with simple eye contact. When Bastien stood, he shook Draper's hand. "Keep her safe." His voice had the note of begging to it, a scared sadness that didn't usually happen when he spoke about Lane. I mean, I knew he cared about her, but he sounded downright woebegone at the thought of leaving Lane behind.

Uncle Henri spat through his cage. "Safe? Do you think Morgan will ever let Rosalie go? She wants to use the girl to find Avalon's lost magic. There's no limit to how far she'll push you to get what she wants. You're as good as caged, once she learns you're here."

Bastien moved over to the prison Henri was mouthing off in, reached his arm inside and jerked Henri hard against the bars, cracking his head four times with force enough to knock out a bull. "That's a good boy," he said as he released Duke Henri, who slumped on the floor, unconscious.

Lane pulled me in for a tight hug, her cold arms doing their best to rally me before I went off to fight my mother. "Do you know who you are?" she whispered.

I nodded. "Most days I think I do."

"You're my daughter, Rosie. I want you to be kind – always kind. I don't want you to have to rely on your strength, but to know that it's there. Never stop being you. You're the best you I know."

I smirked at her cuteness, noting how similar we sounded. "I think I'm the best mini-you you know," I added. "If I grow up to be just like you, then I win at life."

Lane gripped me tighter, her motherly wisdom spilling

out in a rush. "I want you to marry the man of your dreams and get out of Avalon for a while. Promise me you'll smile and be brave, even when it's hard."

I rubbed her back gently. "Of course I will. I love you, Mom. You're the best friend a Spice Girl could have."

Lane snorted, her ribs shaking with silent laughter. "Only you could make me laugh in a dungeon. Only you. You're my best friend, Ro." She squeezed me tighter. "Any idea where Kerdik and Morgan are?"

I checked in with my gut, which was ready to get down to business. "They're on the balcony overlooking the drawbridge at the front of the castle. Fourth floor, I think." I grimaced, my brain flicking through all the things that horrified me. "No. She's torturing them in public now? Making a scene of how powerful she is to be able to control the immortals?"

"Thanks. That's all I needed to know." Then Lane stepped away and nodded to Draper, who wrapped his arms around me from behind in a sweet hug. "I'll be back as soon as I can. Draper, look after your sister. See she gets home safe."

"No problem, Mom."

Panic seized me around the throat when I realized what Lane was planning. "Wait, what? No! You can't kill Morgan, Lane. You're barely upright! Stop!" Draper's arms around me tightened, restraining me from running forward. "Bastien, stop her!"

Bastien didn't turn to Lane, but moved in so I was sandwiched in between him and Draper. His hand moved to my mouth as I thrashed against the two. "Lane's coming with me to end Morgan, and you're staying here. The more noise you make, the higher chance you have of one of the soldiers coming down and blowing our one window to do this." He squeezed his hand over my mouth until I stopped my muffled shouting. "I'll make sure Lane comes back to you. You dying up there is something neither Lane nor I could handle, so this is how it's going down. Say, 'I understand, Bastien.'"

"Bite me, you jag! Don't you dare lock me down here! This is *my* fight. Morgan is *my* mother. You can't take Lane up there! You know the risks!"

"I do, and so does she. This is my call, and you'll accept it. You're going to be my wife, and I won't let you go walking into the lion's den when there's another option. And I won't let you kill your own mother. No matter how much we all know Morgan has to die, it would break your heart to be the one to deliver that final blow. I won't put you through that."

When I was about to spit more vitriol at him, Bastien raised his voice to silence my rant. "This is what my love looks like, Rosie! Don't you understand that if you don't live through this day, there's no point for me? Why are you constantly underestimating how much I need you? I love you even when you hate me." He didn't wait for my answer, but kissed me hard and fast just once before I could bite him in retaliation.

Bastien was the same kind of stubborn as I was, and we shared that unapologetic vicious streak when the people we loved were threatened. I couldn't fault him for it, but I didn't have to comply with the terrible plan, either. "Bastien, no!"

Draper clapped his hand over my mouth as Bastien backed away and Lane opened the door. He met my eyes and blew me a kiss before he left, tucking Lane under his cape at his side before they shut the door behind them.

14

A DUPLEX BUILT FOR NINE

Due to my unwillingness to come close to hurting him in our scuffle, Draper wrestled me to the floor and sat on me like a jerk when I tried to break free. My face was pressed to the cold stone, and Draper was bouncing lightly with his butt atop mine. I didn't cry out for Bastien to change his mind, lest we be found out, but I did struggle and call Draper every nasty name I could think of.

"You forgot 'ingrate'," he suggested, mildly amused at my fight.

"Shut up! It's your mom up there, too. You should be fighting her down here, not me!"

"And yet, here we are." He leaned over and patted my cheek twice, just to piss me off.

I growled at him like an animal, ready to pounce. I'm

not sure why Reyn found this hilarious, but his chuckle was just enough to turn my attention from plotting Draper's painful demise. "Something funny over there, Uncle-Dad?"

"You. You're exactly like your mother." When I snarled at this, he waved off my anger. "Lane, not Morgan. Though, all the Daughters of Avalon are painfully stubborn."

"Yes, how cute it is to not want the woman who raised you to be killed," I simpered, frustrated that Draper was still on top of me. "Would you let me up? I mean, for crying out loud. You weigh a ton!"

Draper bounced a few more times, not acquiescing to my demands. "It's funny because I can't see you. I feel like I'm floating."

"Get up!"

"See? This is what we missed out on when I was stuck in Avalon and you were growing up in Common."

"Oh, the joys of having a sibling."

"Yes. I do all sorts of terrible things, like keep you from death. You've never killed anyone before. I won't have your first kill be your own mother."

"Lane is my mother," I argued, not wanting to tell him that I'd killed before, and recently.

Draper softened. "I know. This was her call, and as her children, we'll respect it. Lane wouldn't go up there unless she knew something we didn't. She can do this."

"Don't you try your optimistic cheerleader shiz on me. I'll straight up beat your butt after this!"

Draper ignored me. "How are you feeling, Reyn?"

Reyn scoffed, as if there wasn't a suitable answer for how crappy this whole situation had turned out. "I'm upright, which is the best thing I can say about it all right now." When I struggled again, Reyn cast me a gentle smile, his darker features barely visible in the flickering lamplight. His kind emerald eyes were clear as day, though, which was how his sweetness usually tended to be. "They'll come back to us."

"Or we'll lose everything! You get that it's pretty much fifty-fifty, right? Am I the only one taking this seriously?"

Reyn studied his fingernails for several long seconds with a compassion that came from experience. "I know your pain," he said quietly. Then he took the conversation in a direction neither of us could've predicted. "You'll be my only children, you know. Lane can't..." He cleared his throat uncomfortably. "So long as I can be with her, that's alright. Still, since you're her daughter, when I marry Lane, you'll be mine, too."

I gaped at him. Though I'd known this and teased him about from time to time, it still felt surreal. "I guess that's true."

"I don't know how to have a daughter, much less one who's already grown." His eyes shifted to Draper. "I've never had a son, much less one so close to my own age."

Draper snorted, and offered a respectful bow of his head. "I wouldn't mind you as a father."

I frowned at Reyn, though he couldn't see it. "I got

news for you, chief, I'm raised already. You're off the hook as far as that goes. I'm only like, eight years younger than you."

Reyn nodded. "If you had a daughter, would you let her go up against someone who wanted to capture her and use her to make the world a worse place?"

"I'm not playing this game with you. Daughter or not, no girl's going to let her best friend walk into a situation where she has to murder her family member. Morgan's already had her brutalized too many times to count. I could've done it."

"But because Lane loves you, now you don't have to."

My anger fell to the wayside as anxiety poked through. "If she doesn't make it... If Bastien doesn't come back... Reyn, I can't take this!"

Reyn motioned for Draper to let me up. "I need to see your face. Come here, Rosie."

I shoved Draper when he rolled off of me, but he only laughed at my anger. I crawled over to Reyn and draped the edge of my cloak over his knee, so he could see me. "Better?"

"I have as much to lose in this as you, but there's nothing we can do about it right now. Sit with your father for a while. I'm not feeling too hot."

I leaned against the wall, turning my head from Draper as he sat down on my other side after shoving Astin's body in the cell he'd previously occupied. My brother lifted a corner of my cape to lay over his thigh, so the three of us could see each other. I worried about Reyn's shallow breaths. I wanted to give him water or something, but I had nothing to offer. "What can I do, Reyn?"

"You can tell me it gets better than this. You can tell me that when I marry Lane and you marry Bastien, we'll start over. Tell me our life in Common won't be a thing like this dungeon."

I reached down and sifted my fingers through his, squeezing his hand. It was musty and dirty in the dungeon, with grime covering the floor and stone walls, but I was determined that Reyn should have something lovely to hold onto. I brought my knees to my chest, cozying in for a dreamy story I was prepared to make up on the fly if it distracted Reyn from his aches. "When we move to Common, I think we should buy a big farmhouse with plenty of land. Like, a few acres, at least. We can make it into a duplex, so we never have to split up."

"What's a duplex?"

"It's a house that's divided down the middle, and inside, both halves contain all the stuff to make up a functional house. So each side has its own kitchen, enough bedrooms and bathrooms and whatnot. If we get a duplex, then we'll have our own space, but we'll still be together."

"Hello, what about me?" Draper said, affronted. "You four will be in your honeymoon stages, and where does that leave me?"

I decided to extend the olive branch and reached out to hold Draper's hand, linking the three of us together more securely. "You, Judah, Link, Mad and Annabelle can stay with either of us. Pick which house you want to live in, and we'll make sure you get a wicked cool bedroom. My dad's going to be visiting a lot, so we might want to earmark a room for him, too." My voice faltered when I was about to suggest we make some space for Kerdik, but I knew Kerdik would never come to Common and risk muting his magic in the exchange. I also knew Bastien wouldn't be cool with that, and truthfully, neither would I. It was time for me to be with one man, no matter how much it hurt to cut that tie that bound me to Kerdik so tightly. Plus, green skin on earth would be a hard sell.

"Where'd you go in your head just then?" Draper wondered aloud.

I shook my head, knowing there would be less harrowing times for such fretting. "When we go to my world, we'll have a whole bunch of animals, obviously. We'll get regular people jobs and we can go to school together, if you guys want. Maybe I'll be able to finish my degree."

Reyn let out a grunt of frustration at the pain his back was in, and shifted uncomfortably next to me. "What else? Keep distracting me."

"Okay, we have to go to this beach by our apartment. It's so gorgeous. I mean, I know you guys are up to your ears in nature here, but this one's got volleyball nets up, picnic tables, grills, a couple waterslides, a biking trail, a fishing pond, a nature center and a basketball court. You could totally spend a whole day there and not see half of it."

"That sounds nice. What's basketball?"

I gaped at Reyn, but quickly remembered my manners. "It's only one of the greatest games. You can hang with people who you don't have to be friends with beforehand if you play basketball together. It's bonding." I started explaining the rules of the game to them, but was cut short when we heard footsteps echoing down the stairwell.

Draper and I moved together without speaking, dragging Reyn away from the door, and into the far corner behind one of the rows of cages. I quietly shut each of the cage doors, so the soldier wouldn't know there'd been a jailbreak right away.

Draper stood next to the door so that when it swung open he would be concealed behind it. Hopefully we could jump the intruder after the door was shut. My brother tucked me behind him, though both of us had our knives drawn. "Stay hidden as long as you can. The second they know you're here, Lane and Bastien won't stand a chance."

I held my breath when the key jangled in the lock. The door swung open, and I wished I hadn't peeked around Draper's shoulder for a look. I knew the back of Rigby's head well – his erect posture and graceful movements.

"Astin? I've come with food for the prisoners." When

his eyes fell on the empty cages, it was already too late for him.

Draper sprang out from the wall and sunk his knife into Rigby's side, cuffing him around the neck with his capable bicep. Draper whispered over his shoulder, "Rosie, shut the door!"

15

MY OWN PERSONAL JUDAS

I was stunned, but managed to obey. My hands were trembling with trepidation, not wanting to be near someone who'd betrayed me so deeply. Despite my big talk that I didn't want to get edged out of the fight, I let Draper handle this one. He lowered Rigby to the stone floor and cuffed his hand over his mouth to stifle any shouting that might alert the rest of the household. Draper leaned over Ribgy's supine body so he could get in his face. "Tell me if Duchess Elaine's been found out up there, and I'll make your death quick."

Rigby gasped as he writhed in pain. Draper didn't uncover his mouth, so Rigby resorted to shaking his head.

"Good. Now tell me how many guards are in the house right now."

Rigby jerked and moaned, tugging on my heartstrings. Draper pulled his hand away for the breathy reply. "Two dozen, though the household staff are well-trained, too. If you're to escape, going out the back is your best bet. Seven guards are there. If you can get past them, you'll be free."

I was shocked Rigby actually told the truth. There had been seven guards out back, which Bastien and I had killed on our way in.

"Are you trying to set us up?" Draper asked with a threat in his tone.

"No. If you let me bleed down here, someone will come for me, and I'll tell them you escaped with plans to disappear into the crowd at the front of the castle." Rigby's breath came in labored pants. "I wasn't supposed to bring you food twice in one day, but I do because I don't want you to die in here!"

Draper's eyes widened. "Why? Why not free us, if you care so much?"

Rigby gripped Draper's flannel as he gasped though his pain. "Because I wronged Duchess Elaine's daughter. I wronged Princess Rosalie, and it's the only way I can find to make her true mother's life easier after all I did." His confession had the desperation of a madman as sweat beaded on Rigby's forehead. "Princess Rosalie loves the Duchess Elaine, so I made sure none of the soldiers took her against her will. I limited the beatings to only happen when Morgan was watching, and lied, telling her they were happening daily."

Draper dropped his hands from Rigby, sitting back on his heels in confusion. "Why would you do that?"

Rigby writhed, touching his side through his red suit jacket to feel the blood.

I knew I was supposed to stay hidden, but I was so stunned, I disregarded the rules. I moved forward and knelt at Rigby's other side, scooping up his hand to warm it. "Hey, Rigs. Did you miss me?"

Rigby's eyes widened when I materialized out of nowhere, looking down on him as if I was his own personal angel of death. "Princess?" He startled, and then scrambled to sit up without much success. "No! You can't be here. Her majesty most high will find you! She'll take you, and then all of Avalon is doomed!"

I shushed him, laying him back down gently and brushing his messed hair from his forehead. I'd envisioned telling off my own personal Judas if I ever saw him again, but seeing him laid out and bleeding all over the floor gave me pause. His confession sounded real, but then, so much of his friendship had fooled me before it all went south. "Morgan won't find me. Morgan's dying today, so you don't have to worry anymore."

"You don't understand! No one can kill her except for her sisters. King Urien confessed Kerdik's protection on the Daughters of Avalon when he was fading years ago." His eyes widened. "Is that where the duchess has escaped to? You have to stop her! Princess, you don't understand. Morgan put a spell on herself! If anyone attacks her, their magic will spill out and she collects it. That's how she's grown so powerful."

I tried to keep my voice gentle, not knowing how close he was to dying. "I know that, actually. Lane and I are both fine with the risk of losing our magic if it saves Avalon. You know how little I give a crap about my own mojo."

"She's got two immortals here. They've both tried to attack her, and their magic spilled out. She keeps trying to scoop it up, but it won't go into her."

I was shocked that Rigby was being so honest. That's why his betrayal had stung so badly; because he'd been a team player up until the end.

Sweat beaded on Rigby's forehead. "You have to leave, Princess. If Morgan finds you, she won't stop until she's got Avalon's lost magic in her hands. She knows you have your Compass because you found the Duchess when she told you Elaine was in the opposite direction. It was a trap, and now you've come here, right where she wants you!" Actual tears streamed down Rigby's face as he clutched my hand with his trembling grip.

Draper shook his head. "This wound's not fatal, Ro. What do you want me to do with him?"

I shook my head. "Dude, I've got no idea. He's right about everything, including that his absence won't go ten minutes without someone coming to look for him. I don't want us to have to kill a bunch of household servants who were taken here against their will, Drape! What do we do?"

Reyn tapped the cage we'd hidden him behind. "Knock him out and put him in here. When the servants come to check on him, do the same thing. We'll fill up the cages so Lane and Bastien are up against far less."

"I like that plan. At least we can help them a little from down here." Draper dragged Rigby to the cage next to Duke Henri's, and used Rigby's keys to lock him inside.

"Why didn't you kill me?" Rigs whispered, his head jerking around to try and see me.

I moved to his cage and reached through the bars to hold onto his hand, letting my face be visible to him once again. I don't know why I let my heart beat with insecurity, or what sort of truth could be found in what might be a total lie, but I had to know. "Was it all fake? You holding me inside my father's room and loosening my corset so I could breathe. Did you mean it?"

Rigby held my hand in his slippery one, the pain making him wince as he tried not to writhe in the cramped space. "It wasn't a lie." He swallowed thickly, meeting my eyes with desperation. "I'll not ask you to forgive me, or understand how little choice I have in my life here, but I will say that I regret every day that has gone by, knowing it's me who made you afraid of the dark."

I closed my eyes and willed myself not to weep. There were too many sad things to choose just one to cry over. "How could you do that to me? You let them take my clothes and throw me into a well!"

His eyes were fixed on mine, determined to say his piece. "It wasn't until then that I had to face the jaded man

I'd become. Do with me as you wish. I deserve a swift death at your hands for what I did to you."

I didn't contradict him, but let the judgment crackle in the air between us. "You could've obeyed Morgan and still done something, but you left me to rot."

Rigby looked stunned. "Is that what you think? That second day, I tried to sneak you food. Morgan caught me. She had me beaten and locked me in this very dungeon until you were rescued. I tried to help you after the wretched thing I did, but I couldn't get to you!"

Draper took in the tenor of my shock. "You want to redeem yourself? Then tell us how to free Master Kerdik and Brìghde."

Rigby shook his head. "You'd have to return their magic back to them, but it's not possible. Morgan's been using dark spells, perverting normal magic until it bends to her will. Even if you do return it to them, the moment they're free, they'd attack her and their magic would fall out all over again."

Draper covered his mouth at the insider information, and how easy it was to make Rigby spill all the royal secrets. "Well, you'll rot down here, just as you left Rosie to do in the well, and just as you left me, Reyn and Lane, too. Rosie, get back from his cage."

I listened, confused at how twisted everything had become. "You broke my heart," I confessed in whisper.

"Yes, I imagine that's true. I also broke the heart you

restored in me when you moved into this awful place. I loathe myself for all I did to you."

"Good," Reyn rasped. "You'll remember that pain and wear it around your neck every day for the rest of your shortened life. Remember that you almost murdered the Lost Daughter of Avalon."

There was one more thing I wanted to know, but felt stupid asking him in front of the guys. I moved back to the cage, knelt down and whispered, "Was Demi a lie, too?"

Rigby mulled over my words, his hand cupping his side as he choked on his pain. "At first, yes. He was sent to you with no choice in the matter, instructed to make you comfortable. Eventually he was supposed to seduce you into telling him if you still had your Compass ability." Rigby held my gaze. "After the second day, he came to me and confessed that he couldn't do it. That I had to find you a new *soumettre*, because he wouldn't turn you in if he found out."

I closed my eyes and nodded, grateful I could make peace with that uncertainty. "Thank you. Even if you're lying, I needed to hear that."

"It's not a lie. Morgan made him stay your *soumettre* because she saw you had feelings for him. Abusing Demi to make you comply is a trigger she enjoys pulling. But do not doubt that Demi adored you. He drew sketches of your face and wrote you poems while you slept. He kept them tucked inside the books he would read to you. He always hoped you would find them, but I'm guessing you never went snooping through his book."

My voice was small when I finally spoke. "He wrote me poems?"

"I put his book away in my things so no one would find it. It's in the servants' quarters, in a box marked 'Storage'. If you live through this somehow, it's yours."

"Thank you." I moved my hand into the cage to brush my fingers against Rigby's crimson knuckles, but he jerked them away.

"No," Rigby snapped, his rebuke firm. "I don't deserve kindness from you. Do not forgive me. This cage is a just punishment, as is the knife in my side."

"You won't get any arguments from me." Draper crossed his arms over his chest with a stalwart expression on his face.

There was never really a great time for me to switch realities and flip to seeing through Kerdik's eyes, but in front of an outsider was really not the best timing. The dungeon faded from my view, and I called with a quaky note in my voice for Draper, who moved me away from Rigby's cage. His arms were around me, offering comfort while I tried not to panic.

Thousands and thousands of people called for my head. No. Not *my* head, but Kerdik's. He was cuffed to the balcony, on all fours and seething. He willed his magic to return to him, so he could destroy Province 1 in a fit of fiery rage. Blood dripped down his forehead, but it only fueled his fury.

I screamed as the whip cracked down hard across my back – not my back, I tried to remind myself, but Kerdik's. The wounds weren't real, but the pain surely was. I felt Draper trying to soothe me, his hand over my mouth so I didn't alert more soldiers.

Kerdik's head turned to the side and I saw Brìghde, passed out on the floor of the balcony. She was a bloody mess of limbs, her mossy dress dripping with cherry-colored gore. Though I knew Kerdik despised her for his curse, there was a camaraderie that rose up in his throat at the sight of his equal so utterly thrashed.

His chin was jerked up by a rough hand, so the crowd could get a better look at the all-powerful being so defeated. They shouted for his demise, blaming him for every single problem Avalon had ever been through.

"Give me the lost magic, and I'll set you free," Morgan called out from behind him. She didn't sound out of breath at all, so I'm guessing she was having one of her soldiers deliver the beatings.

Kerdik spat over his shoulder in her direction. "That's the thing about mortals. You can whip me until the day you die, but I'll never crack. I'll outlive you, break free and bury you as you lived – alone and dissatisfied." Then he turned to the crowd and shouted, "All of you!"

Morgan shrieked for another beating to be adminis-tered. I winced, though Kerdik did not. I could hear him chanting in his mind that it was just pain, and pain was temporary. He did not have hopes of being rescued, but only of enduring until Morgan gave up.

Twenty lashes of the whip made me choke into Draper's hand with untold agony. My own bloody tears plagued my eyes, but my psychic vision was still intact. I could hear Draper freaking out, but something distracted me when the lashings stopped. It was that sixth sense that tingled my spine when Bastien was in the room. I could feel him nearby, only he wasn't in the dungeon.

Bastien the Bold was somewhere on the balcony.

16

LANE'S ASSAULT AND KERDIK'S PROTECTION

Bastien's invisibility cloak made him impossible to get a visual on, but when the guard whipping Kerdik dropped dead, I knew it was my guy who had shown up to save the day. There were three soldiers on the balcony that I could see, and now two of them were panting through their last breaths as they collapsed at their queen's feet.

Morgan shrieked and ordered for more soldiers.

But I knew they wouldn't come, because I knew Bastien. He would start by cutting off the backup plan, and then move in for the kill – setting his trap before striking. He was patient like that, and just psychotic enough to attempt a government coup in front of an entire province.

Kerdik glanced over his shoulder in confusion as the third soldier hit the ground. Morgan snatched up the fallen whip to arm herself, inviting her attacker with a sneer. "If it's me you came for, let my people see you fall when you try to kill me. Show your face!"

I called for Lane to get back when she stepped out from Bastien's cloak, making it look like she was the one who vanquished the soldiers alone. She had a knife clutched in her weak hand, but a fire in her eyes that made me rally. "Here I am, Morgan. You throw me into your dungeon to rot? Well, you'll have to try a lot harder than that."

Lane didn't bother with a long monologue – the roar of the crowd had grown so deafening, her words couldn't be heard anyway. Instead she lunged, plunging her knife as hard as she could, but missing her mark. Morgan had been feasting while Lane had been trapped in a cage. The knife stabbed Morgan's shoulder, which was a definite point for our team, but as far as victories went, we were miles from our goal.

My stomach roiled when Morgan drew back the whip and brought it down across Lane's face. My best friend in the world belted out a scream I could've gone my whole life never hearing. She stumbled back and fell next to Kerdik, holding her bloody face instead of her knife. Though Kerdik's wrists were still cuffed to the balcony, his leg reached out and drew Lane toward him, cocooning her under the tent of his body to shield her from further harm. My heart clenched in my chest at the kindness and utter selflessness Kerdik exhibited for my Lane. "Aim your whip at me, you witch!" Kerdik bellowed.

"What a fine idea." She cracked Kerdik across the shoulder. "Tell me where the lost magic is!"

Kerdik's chest heaved, but instead of looking downward, he tilted his chin to the sky. Frustration filled him when he studied the cloud of green and silver that congregated above the balcony. It was a feathery, translucent mass that hovered above them just out of reach. "When I retrieve my magic, you will feel the sting of this whip until your sister puts you out of your misery!" I could feel him straining against his cuffs, trying to reach the cloud that was about seven feet above Morgan's head.

Morgan looked up as well, the same frustration at not being able to grab onto Brìghde's and Kerdik's elusive power tugging at her features. Then she lashed out in anger and whipped Kerdik again, while he shielded Lane with his body.

It was then I knew we would soon be on the losing side. Bastien was there, but he couldn't hurt Morgan without his magic falling out. He wasn't qualified to deliver the final blow, and though Lane was, she was incapacitated enough not to be able to finish the job.

I yanked myself out of Kerdik's head, though my tears had clouded my vision too much to see the dim dungeon. "Water! Draper, I can't see!"

My sweet brother didn't have water, so instead he used the shirt Bastien had loaned him, mopping up my face until I could see his furrowed eyebrows again. The story tumbled out of me as I gripped my knife and stood. "I'm going, or we're all toast. Lane's about to die, Draper. I saw it with my own two eyes – or Kerdik's eyes anyways. I'm the backup plan, and Plan A is out the window."

Draper stood with his chest puffed. "Then I'm going with you."

"If you leave, Reyn will get discovered by any of the soldiers who come down here to check. There's nothing you can do as far as taking Morgan down, anyway. It's me or Lane, and Lane's down for the count."

Draper made to protest, but I didn't leave room for an argument. I ignored Rigby's cries of fear and ran for the door, shutting it tight behind me. With my knife clutched firmly in my hand, I glided up the steps, letting my gut lead me to my mothers.

17

A LITTLE GIRL AND HER MOTHER

Hearing the crowd through Kerdik's ears was nothing compared to the real thing. I could barely hear myself think as Morgan kicked at Kerdik while he was chanting words of encouragement to Lane. I stood in the room that had five dead soldiers littering the floor, courtesy of Bastien. At this point, it might as well have been flower petals he'd scattered on the floor to welcome me – so sweet was his protective nature for my family.

I stood in the divide between the empty room and the balcony, letting the wind hit my face and erase the dank stank of the dungeon. Though I was invisible, I knew Bastien could see me since we were both wearing our cloaks. I ducked behind a portion of the wall, hoping Bastien wouldn't see me and give away my location.

My eyes were drawn to Kerdik's back as I peered around the edge of the doorway. His skin was more red than green. "No!" I whispered, gaping at the damage I wanted to turn away from. Of all the things I wished for Kerdik, a life far from all of this was top of the list.

I watched Bastien creep around the perimeter of the balcony. When he used his knife to break Kerdik's bindings, only I understood why Kerdik vanished from view. Screeches of fear from below permeated the evening air when their victim du jour disappeared before their very eyes. Kerdik reappeared a handful of seconds later, uncuffed and furious.

"I can boost you up there!" I heard Bastien yell to Kerdik from my left. He had to shout to be barely heard above the crowd.

Morgan's smile was forced through the pain of her stab wound. "Is that Bastien the Bold? How I would love to get a piece of an Untouchable's magic."

Bastien was moving from his place so Morgan didn't provoke him to attack her. If she could make his magic topple out, it would be hers for the taking. I inched closer, knowing I had one shot to get this right.

Images of what I must've looked like as a baby flooded my mind. The sketch Kerdik had drawn of my parents, smiling hopefully out at the world with me in their arms, was stuck in my brain. It juxtaposed in irreconcilable ways when compared against the woman who was taunting my fiancé with a whip in her fist. Though I knew this was the job, I didn't want it. I'd run from Draper to claim the spot of second in line to get the task done, but now that I was here, my hands trembled with inexperience. The vulnerability I felt in my mother's presence made me feel like a child.

Bastien was trying to keep Kerdik from falling over, and didn't see me move onto the balcony with my knife at the ready. Another step forward, and I was only two feet behind my mother.

"Too green," she jeered, motioning to Kerdik's bare chest when he reappeared and leaned on the balcony as Bastien tended to Lane. "I like you much better covered in red."

That was all it took to remind me that I wasn't a scared child, but a woman on a mission. When Morgan's wrist swung back in preparation for a hearty blow against my barely upright guy, I snatched at the whip and yanked it out of her hand. "That's enough!" I yelled, kicking her knees out from behind and tugging on her hair so she toppled backwards and cracked her head on the stone. "Bastien, boost Kerdik up!"

"I told you to stay put!" Bastien shouted at me as his head whipped around to scowl in my direction. He ultimately obeyed, moving the unsteady Kerdik over to the wall for leverage.

Morgan vanished from the crowd as I climbed atop her supine body, making us both invisible. She gasped as she took in my focused face and the knife in my hand. "Wait!"

"Your adventure ends tonight. I'm done waiting for you to love me!" I yelled, and then plunged the knife down into her chest. I closed my eyes against her screams that I knew my brain would never forget. There was part of my soul that I hadn't known still believed in Santa Claus. A small part of my childlike self hoped that there were fairies who could fly, and mothers who loved their daughters for no good reason. That precious part of my psyche splintered off and withered as my mother's screech finally died on her lips. My right hand started stinging, but I paid it no mind.

I felt something leave me, and guessed that what little magic I had was floating around me somewhere. I didn't care; all that mattered was that no one would whip the people I loved ever again. My hands slipped on the knife I left stuck in my mother's breast, and though I knew there would be tears aplenty in the future, I didn't shed a single one as I reached out and closed her stunned eyes.

My right hand started itching, and then the discomfort grew until it felt like my ring finger was on fire. I looked down, and beneath the shock I was in at murdering my own mother, my aquamarine stone fogged over with a black cloudiness that confused me. "What the..." I shook my hand as if that would do something, but the burning sensation coursed through my body, making me tingle with an ominous darkness that didn't belong in nature, or in me.

18

THE DARKNESS I DIDN'T MEAN TO DO

I heard Bastien's oofs as he lifted Kerdik up so they could snatch at his magic after he'd retrieved mine for me. The sun was setting, giving them no help at all to light the way.

Lane crawled over to me, feeling around until she touched the hem of my cape, inviting herself into my haze of confusion. She gasped at Morgan, who was finally and completely dead. Lane's face was dripping with blood from a deep gouge that went from the right side of her forehead all the way across her nose, and onto the left corner of her chin.

"She hurt you!" I choked out, knowing I couldn't lose it now.

"Shh," Lane cooed. "She'll never hurt us again."

"I killed my mother," I confessed, though that much

was painfully obvious. "They're all going to know that I killed my mother."

After all the horrors she'd been through, Lane only worried about me. She threw her arms around my shoulders and pried me off of Morgan's body. "So help me, this will not be your adventure! You are meant for more than this life!" Rage made her arms shake as she kissed my forehead. "Wait over here, baby. I'll take care of it. No one will ever know if you stay invisible." Then she grabbed Morgan's ankle and dragged her over to the edge of the balcony, standing to address the people who had called for more and more blood.

The jeers fell away in the twilight, and a crack of fear rippled through the crowd as Bastien gave up on helping Kerdik, and moved over to help Lane heft up Morgan's body, balancing it on the railing overlooking the entire province. Then he stepped back so the whole land could see Lane – fierce in all her glory as blood dripped down her face.

Lane's voice was strong, though the rest of her was faltering. "Province 1 is no more! I killed your queen, which means this land is mine! All of you belong to me now, but I don't want a single one of you! Province 10 is closed to you and your families. Fend for yourselves, which is what you left the other provinces to do! Morgan's jewels belong to me now, and I'm giving them back to Master Kerdik, who you mocked! See how well he favors you now! You begged for his pain? Now you can beg for his mercy!" When cries of horror and anguish wove through the crowd, Lane shouted, "You put your hope in one woman, not in Avalon, and here she is. You wanted her? Well, you can have her!" Lane tore the rings off her sister's fingers and pushed her off the balcony, eliciting a mass scream from the crowd as Morgan le Fae fell into the moat four stories below. "Morgan le Fae was your greatest adventure, and now she is over."

I was in utter shock and horror, but that was soon replaced by the pain of my finger lighting itself on fire. Like, actual fire. I shouted for Bastien to help me.

He swore at the sight only the two of us could see. "How did you do that?"

"I don't know!" I smothered the small flame in my shirt, biting my lip through a scream of pain at the burned skin being roughed up. "I have to get this thing off me!"

But it was too late for that. Kerdik shouted, "No!" as a black and purple fog shot out of my ring and thrust itself out into the air, aiming for the crowd, who was scattering from Lane's wrath. "The lost magic is spilling out!"

The black and purple began to dissipate from the cloudy mass, forming into raindrops that trickled down on the people, making them scream as if the black rain burned their skin. Some fell on their faces and tore at their clothes, howling in agony at the sky.

"Bastien, help me! I need my magic now!" Kerdik cried as he stumbled toward me, reaching in the air for my body, which he couldn't see.

Bastien dove into the backroom and hefted out a chair, grabbing Kerdik by the arm and lifting him up as he climbed atop the seat. The extra two feet were all Kerdik needed to finally be able to jump up and reclaim what was rightfully his. He cried out with ecstasy that mingled with anguish as his immeasurable powers reentered his body. He stood straight as his body began to repair itself, like a doll being sewn back together.

The feathery cloud above him was only silver now, since he'd retrieved the green magic for himself. When he stretched out his limbs and found they had vitality again, he scooped up Brìghde from the floor and threw her up into the air above the balcony with strength that belied his bloodied form. Her body punched through the silver haze, bursting feather-like wisps everywhere, and reviving her with a cry of shock as she finally came to. The silver absorbed into her body, as if she was a sponge sucking in water. She landed in a pile of limbs, but this time she was able to pick herself up. Vengeance sparked in her bright blue eyes as she took in her surroundings with renewed strength and focus. Her flaming red hair was matted with blood, making her look that much more lethal. Legit storm clouds moved in, making it difficult to pick out the black and purple fog that had shot from my ring. Brìghde could control the weather, which was exactly the turn her wrath was taking. Buckets of rain burst down on the land as she howled out her rage, soaking us all in ten seconds flat. "Where is she? Where is Avalon's Queen of the Fae?"

"Dead," Lane croaked out. For how cool she normally played most things, I could tell being downwind from an Éirish immortal was a new one for her. "She'll never come for you again."

"Kerdik, your ring!" I called out, untying my cape so he could see me. I needed him to know that I was ground zero for the black fog. "It's freaking out!"

When he saw my scared face, his shock couldn't be concealed. He lunged for me, muttering frantically in a language I didn't understand as he put his palm over my ring. The black fog stopped oozing from my gemstone finally, and we both heaved a sigh of relief, though the acid rain was still in full effect out on the grounds. After the elation settled, Kerdik was livid. "I told you not to come here! Are you so bent on defiance that you can't follow simple instructions?"

"You were being beaten! Am I supposed to sit back and do nothing while you're in pain?"

"Yes! Yes, that's exactly what you're supposed to do."

Rain dripped down my face, but it didn't mar any of the devotion in my eyes. "I would never leave you to fend for yourself like that! The fact that you think I'm capable of it shows how blind you are."

Kerdik stopped short, rain trailing down his features, washing some of the blood off in streaks. He blinked a few times, as if confused that the hold I had on him went both ways. Then he looked out at the angry sky with taut lips. "Blind, perhaps, but you don't understand what you've done. My suffering isn't worth what you've unleashed!"

My nose scrunched. "What are you talking about?"

"Your ring! You're the one who killed Morgan le Fae? She strengthened her protection so that anyone who tried to attack her would have all their magic fall out. Your ring, Rosie! Your ring is where I hid Faîte's lost magic."

I paled, swiping the rain from my eyes as I turned my head from staring at Kerdik to studying the black and purple cloud in confusion. "Morgan's magic isn't stronger than all of Faîte's lost mojo. That isn't what's happening."

"The people are becoming infected with the lost magic!" Kerdik shouted in fear.

I touched my forehead in consternation. "Do you think that's possible? I mean, can you call it back?"

"Not when it's exposed and raw like this. Not all of it, anyways." Kerdik met my eyes, his accusations and frustration dying down when he saw my fear, and the love that drove me to risk it all to save him. "You came for me."

"Of course I did."

"You love me."

The passion in my eyes blazed like a fire crackling between us. "I do."

Kerdik stood and quickly explained to his immortal friend-slash-enemy what was happening. Brìghde's face vacillated from shock to betrayal to fear. The black and purple was spreading out under her storm clouds, the droplets of inky paint infecting Avalon's worst with who knows what kind of magical steroids. Thunder sounded overhead, adding the edge of urgency to our worst fear realized.

After a back and forth between the two immortals that I didn't hear, due to the screams of the crowd below, Kerdik and Brìghde braced themselves by leaning forward on the balcony. Together they raised their palms out, as if conducting a symphony that was too dark for Mozart. They were bloody yet serene in their calculated fury. It was almost beautiful... until it turned into a massacre.

Lightning and giant rocks shot out from their palms, hitting with purposeful aim the residents who had laughed at their hopelessness. It was a brutal video game, shooting the bad guys with lasers and watching them vaporize or fall dead, with a hole torn clean through their bodies. The rocks hit them in the heads so hard, I knew they wouldn't be getting back up.

"What did ye do?" Brìghde accused Kerdik, not taking her eyes off her prey.

"It doesn't matter now. It's done."

"After all this time, how is this happening here?"

Kerdik flicked his wrist and sent a boulder flinging out sideways, plunging it down into a whole mess of people as it rolled and gained momentum. They ran from the monster they'd thought was a beaten dog, but they couldn't escape fast enough.

Kerdik lowered his chin. "I hid the magic with the mortal woman I told you about. She didn't know, and when she killed Morgan to avenge us just now, the darkness spilled out."

How Brìghde managed a snarky smile was beyond me, but girlfriend was on top of her game after being healed so rapidly. "Ah, did your doll survive? Is tha her?" She motioned to Lane, who was studying the black fog with a worried expression.

"She survived, but that's not her. Focus on the fog, not the people. We have to call it back!"

"How? We haven't done this in ages, Kerdik!"

"Bastien?" he called over his shoulder. "Take Rosie into the castle, but no further than the room there. We'll try to harness the magic and put it back in her ring, but it might take some time." Then his tone turned sharp. "Brìghde! You're losing your end! If the black fog slips from us, it'll migrate to Éireland. Your people can't handle the challenge of going back to the way things were. Focus!"

Bastien didn't bother waiting for me to stand on clumsy legs, but scooped me up and ran me into the room that was littered with the bodies of dead soldiers. "Did you know that would happen?" Bastien demanded, almost in accusation.

"What? Of course not! Why would I send evil mojo back into Faîte? I just wanted Morgan taken out. Everything else is a blur." My eyes searched out his in my confusion. "Did I really do it? Did I murder my own mother?"

Bastien drew me to him, holding me to his chest. "Let's not think about that right now. What matters is we're safe."

I pointed out the doorway into the rainy sky that had swirls of black and purple now darting through it, like snakes on a mission. Instead of just rain and clouds, the fog seemed sentient somehow, like it knew it was being hunted. It slipped as fast as it could toward the home Kerdik and the other immortals had yanked it from so long ago. "Did I really do that? Did I just kill a monster only to make hundreds more?"

"No," Bastien cooed, though I could hear the doubt in his tone. "I'm sure Kerdik and Brìghde are handling it. They'll fix it. Hey," he turned my chin so my frightened eyes were staring into his. "I'm here. The worst is over, now that Morgan's gone."

Wails like I'd never heard before erupted from female mouths. I expected mourning and sobbing, but this was different. These screeches had a grating, metallic sound behind their operatic, nonsensical yelling. I cringed and clapped my hands over my ears, trying desperately to keep up.

I saw Bastien's fear that the magic I'd set loose was doing something freaky. The screams weren't like anything I'd heard before. It bespoke the beginning of the end.

I heard animalistic growling, and then fearful cries beneath the ear-piercing wails that seemed to stretch on forever. I watched Bastien's mouth swear over and over at the scene I couldn't see, what with his body blocking my view. When I tried to step forward to look, Bastien's arm shot around me and secured me to his chest. "Lane!" he called. When she didn't turn from her perch, Bastien picked up a piece from a splintered chair that had been bashed during the scuffle and chucked it at her. When she turned around, he motioned her to his side.

With tears streaming down her torn face, Lane stumbled into the room." Get down!" she warned. The moment we obeyed, she collapsed on her knees to put her arms around us. "Banshees!" she clarified, though I didn't so much know what that was. She pointed to her ears to indicate the incessant screaming, which was thankfully starting to fade to a more acceptable decibel. "There haven't been banshees in Avalon... maybe ever! Banshees are from Éireland, but they've been extinct for years. The lost magic is latching onto the people," she said to Bastien with trepidation tauter than a violin's string.

Bastien kept one arm around me and wrapped the other around Lane, pulling her to his side in a hug she desperately needed. "There's nothing we can do right now. This is all for Kerdik and Brìghde to deal with."

Lane's tears flowed freely, now that there was a shoulder strong enough to hold her burdens. "She used to braid my hair," Lane confessed, reaching out across Bastien and clutching my hand with closed eyes. "Every morning, Morgan would French braid my hair and turn it into a crown of braids. My sister's dead, and the worst part is that it's a good thing she finally died. How sucky is that?" Lane broke down while Bastien held her.

"Keep the good parts of her," I suggested, squeezing

Lane's elbow. "The parts of Morgan only you and Dad knew. Those are the parts of her that get to live. When this all blows over, you're going to crown-braid my hair, and that's the part of Morgan we keep."

Lane met my eyes, her mangled face latching onto that one fragment of hope she desperately needed. Finally, she nodded. "I like that idea." Her eyes flicked to Bastien's, worry etched deeper than the marks I prayed wouldn't be too permanent. "If the banshees are out, the others will come. Their screams announce death, Bastien. If there are banshees in Avalon..."

The sentence hung in the air while we clung to each other, unfinished as we feared the worst.

19

WORTH IT ALL

Kerdik and Brìghde were livid and in hyper-concentration-mode, which meant the weather was going berserk and the castle walls were shaking. The rain fell hard, blowing sideways and making us shiver in the doorway where we were huddled. When the rain started mixing with sleet, the ice chunks were too volatile to be near, so we moved a few feet further inside. Lane had tears streaming down her ripped face, understanding more of the gravity of what was going on than I did. "Where are Reyn and Draper?"

"In the dungeon with Rigby. They're okay."

"You should've stayed down there!" she yelled, trying to be heard over the whipping wind. She was also pretty worked up, so her temper was swinging. "When I tell you to do something, that's the only thing you should be trying to do!"

"I saw through Kerdik's eyes that you couldn't even stand! What was I supposed to do? I wasn't about to pop myself some popcorn and watch Morgan murder you! Screw being obedient! I won't let you die!"

"My life isn't worth unleashing all the dark magic back into the world, Ro."

It was like she'd slapped me. "Is that what you think? Do you think people like you come around every day? That just anyone would up and leave a castle and a crown to raise a baby as a homeless teenager? You're one of the few good things left in this terrible place!"

Lane lunged around Bastien and clutched me tight, knocking the wind out of me. "You were worth it all."

I shrieked, ending the tender moment when bowling ball-sized chunks of ice started falling from the heavens. In addition to well-aimed bolts of lightning, the hail was knocking people out left and right. Brìghde was cackling madly as the clouds gathered in a swirl across the sky, trying to catch the black fog that was desperately trying to escape. When snake-like threads started to bleed out of the swirl and sneak into the further reaches of the sky, Brìghde shrieked for Kerdik to help her.

Kerdik didn't waste a second, but scooped her to stand in front of him, her spine tight to his chest. He pressed his palms to the backs of her hands, bracing them both for a double shot of the good stuff. They aimed their hands toward the swirl, widening the radius so it took up more real estate in the sky. Brìghde cried out as if she was still being tortured, but Kerdik was unswerving in his focus.

When snow started falling from the sky like the most peaceful Christmas in the midst of all the chaos, my eyes darted through the partly dead and partly fleeing crowd. I don't know how she knew when to come, but somehow there she was. Cailleach was using her cane, hobbling through the chaos as if she was on a peaceful evening stroll through town. She was the mid-thirties beauty to me, though I knew now that everyone else saw her as the hag she'd been marketed as. Her eyes were focused on the black snakes that were leaching through the sky. Every now and then she lifted her cane to shoot a lightning bolt at them, trapping a few and yanking the dodgy wisps into her cane. Her lightning wasn't traditional like Brìghde's, but instead had a blue line of ice to it.

Lane's voice was fearful. "Is that... Is that Cailleach?"

I nodded. "She's the one who helped us get here. I told her to stay away until Morgan was killed. Not bad timing, actually."

"Cailleach is in Avalon?" Lane's voice held a note of fear and reverence to it as her head craned to study the woman with blue dread locks whipping behind her in the wind. "We're either saved, or we're all going to die."

Brìghde's screams of agony were reaching a fever pitch, so Cailleach decided she was done with her leisurely stroll. She vanished, and then reappeared seconds later on the balcony with a softness to her step. "You're finished," she ruled, waving her cane to the two immortals, who were winded and bloody.

Kerdik collapsed, his knees buckling as Brìghde fell backward atop him. I ignored Lane and Bastien's cries for me to stay put and scrambled to get to Kerdik. I was careful with Brìghde as the sleet fell on her bloodied body. I rolled her off and brushed her hair out of her face before Cailleach gently shooed me away so she could tend to her sister.

I flung myself across Kerdik's chest. Before tears could overtake me, I sat up and scooped his shoulders to rest on my lap. His lashes were fluttering with weakness, making my heart stutter. I debated between shaking him and cradling him gently, unsure which would be more effective. I lightly slapped his cheek to help him focus. "Kerdik? Honey, talk to me."

"It's escaping!" he moaned, lifting his hand to point to the sky. His weighted arm quickly collapsed, scaring me with how frail he was.

"Tell me how to help. What can I do?"

Kerdik's gaze flitted around before it fell on me. The hardness and haziness melted away when he focused on my features. "You're here."

My heart broke for the isolation he was so used to. "Of course I'm here. We all came to help you. I wasn't about to let Morgan get away with hurting you. You're my..."

Kerdik looked at me as if I was the sun, the moon and

the stars, all congregating to shine just for him. "You love me."

I closed my eyes and lifted him a little further so I could press his cheek to mine. "It's all over. She'll never hurt you again." I rocked him as if he was my baby. He could command nature and do any number of impossible things, yet he was vulnerable and pliable in my arms. "I won't let anyone beat you like that as long as I live. Don't you worry. I'm here."

With our cheeks pressed together, no one heard his confession when he let himself unload to me. "I haven't felt physical pain in so long; I underestimated the madness it can drive a man to. Don't let me destroy Avalon," he begged, his fingers fumbling to rest in mine, as if to hand me a portion of his vengeance.

"I'll keep you safe," I promised. "You don't want to destroy Avalon. There are good people still left in it. Think of Urien, and how much you love him."

Kerdik nodded into my neck. "Tell me more things like that."

"You protected Lane. You took a few lashings that were meant for her." I moved my cheek up and down, savoring the intimacy I knew would have to go away soon. "If you thought Avalon wasn't worth saving, you wouldn't have gone to such lengths to rescue my Lane." My voice was just loud enough for him to hear above the sleet that pelted us and made me shiver against him. "I see the goodness inside your heart, Kerdik. I see you, and I love you."

His fingers went limp in my hand, his struggle over whether or not to destroy it all and start from scratch finally coming to a crest. "You'll be Bastien's princess for now, but when you're my queen, I want Avalon to be a safer place for us. I have to help Brighde gather up the higher magic!" He struggled to sit up straight, but couldn't. With a groan of frustration, he collapsed back into my tender hold.

My insides warmed at the goodness I'd always known was in him. I knew I should've shut down all conversation about our future, but after being driven to the brink as we were, I indulged us both in a little foolishness. "I'd like that. Where will we live?"

Kerdik's lashes fluttered against my face, his lips tickling my ears. "I'll build you a castle, and we'll fill it with babies. The whole land will smell like a haven because I'll fill it with every color rose you can think of."

I knew I should've run from the conversation we shouldn't be having, but my lips let out a traitorous chuckle. "I think that sounds nice. Can our kids be green? I think that'd be cool."

Kerdik stilled, and then his chest seemed to swell, his lifetimes of insecurities falling to the wayside. When his voice came out, there was a tremulous wonder of unshed tears just barely held back from spilling over. "You want our children to look like me?"

"I do. Can we build a little treehouse for our kids to have adventures in? I always wanted one of those."

I felt Kerdik's smile lift my cheek. "We can have anything you like. A treehouse for every day of the week."

The mood shifted as the wind whipped at my clothes. "And you'll let me go until then? You'll let me be happy with Bastien until it's our time?"

Kerdik's hand balled into a fist as his body stiffened. "I can do that for you. Only promise you'll come back to me."

"My very best promise."

Cailleach and Brìghde were arguing, now that Brìghde was revived enough with Cailleach's help. "It has to be gathered back!"

Cailleach shrugged, as if she couldn't care less about Brìghde's fear. "Does it? After what they did to ye? I think they should contend with real darkness, so they can see what a fight should truly look like. Look at what happened here with no dark magic at all. Idle hands look for mischief. I want to see what happens when they're so turned around, capturing us is the last thing on their minds."

"You're unleashing Vampires in Avalon!"

Cailleach raised an eyebrow. "Tha ye think I care what happens to Avalon amuses me." She pointed to the black snakes that were skittering from the fog across the sky and heading east. "I want to see Éireland restored to her former days of more magic than anyone knew what to do with. They can't even turn invisible anymore! Let the children have their fun. Let the madness come."

Kerdik turned his face from mine to shout through the

wind at Cailleach. "We agreed years ago that neither of our lands could handle that much magic!"

Cailleach didn't bother to look at him as she spoke, but watched the tumult of the oversized hail as it cracked down on the injured and dying below. "Yes, but times have changed. They're so desperate to get their hands on power tha they'll kidnap two immortals to get at it. Let them have what they want." Her eyes narrowed at the people in the throes of a war brought down on their heads by nature herself. "Let them burn for it."

20

CONVINCING CAILLEACH

Brighde kept trying to wrangle the dark magic with her cloud vortex, ignoring her sister who didn't think the world was worth saving.

Bastien braved the storm and hefted Kerdik up to take him inside to safety, motioning with a jerk of his chin for me to follow him inside. The cold made my joints inflexible and my jaw tight, but it had been worth it to make sure Kerdik was alright. Bastien's arms went around my torso to warm me and steady my uncertain footsteps.

Lane crawled her way to Kerdik, her movements stiff and careful. "You saved my life," she remarked quietly, leaning him forward to check his back. "I can't believe how seamless that looks. Like it never even happened."

He met her eyes, showing her the rare flash of vulnerability he usually only revealed to me. "But it did happen. Over and over."

Her eyes closed, as if feeling his pain. "I know. Why did you do it? Why did you save me?"

"Because I love your daughter, and she loves you."

Lane lowered her chin, letting the words sizzle in the air. I knew Bastien had heard, but it was no secret anymore. Still, Bastien remained in place with his arms around me, treacherous though I was to give my heart to two men.

Cailleach moved inside, while Brìghde contented herself with her angry cloud tornado from the balcony. She pointed her staff at Kerdik with a stern arch in her eyebrow. "Ye went after my Brìghde to save her. I'll not forget tha."

Kerdik's reply came back distraught as he struggled with the simple act of breathing. "My curse, Cailleach. I need you to remove my curse! I've paid for my sins long enough."

Cailleach's gaze flicked to me, and a smile played on her wrinkled, sultry lips. No doubt they looked wrinkly to everyone else, but to me she was a beauty queen. I'm not sure why that made her smile that much more terrifying, but I shrank back from the vindictive nature of her happiness. "Oh, but what fun is a curse tha can be undone?"

"Undo my curse!" Kerdik bellowed, and the castle walls shook with his temper.

Lane scurried away, crashing into Bastien's arm that welcomed her into our huddle. The three of us were vanished with our robes, on the periphery of an immortals' quarrel.

It was then that the remnants of the soldiers decided it would be a fine idea to try their hands at avenging their queen. Six men barged in, armed and wide-eyed with a death wish. Bastien moved us to the corner and drew his knife, ready to fight his former brothers-in-arms.

Cailleach rolled her eyes at the intrusion, and flicked her wrist to raise up a thick wall of ice to separate us from the fray. Bastien howled, though it didn't seem to be from pain, but more anger that he'd been cut off from us. My pulse climbed, but Bastien turned with a sudden calmness, as if ready for a fight that could be all his.

The immortals were unperturbed, and carried on their heated conversation as if there had been no interruption. Cailleach's voice was sharp as she barked at Kerdik. "How many women would ye ruin if I were to lift your curse? How many would trust ye, only to be left feeling foolish after ye showed your true colors?"

"One woman would know me, and I would never leave her." Kerdik's furious promise made my heart ache.

The black in the sky was slipping through Brìghde's fingers as she shrieked, but it seemed the world and all of its problems were fading from my focus. I could see only Kerdik, and hear his pledge that existed only for me.

Cailleach's eyes cut to me, giving me a knowing look that had a smirk of mischief to it. "Very well. If ye want your curse lifted so ye can be with this girl, then that's what ye shall have."

Kerdik stiffened, and then scrambled to his feet to stand, swaying with the weight of everything he'd endured. His movements were janky and unfocused as he fought with gravity. He didn't seem to feel the cold, but only the possibility that his isolation might not be permanent. He gripped Cailleach's gray robes with an unhinged craze in his eyes. "Are you truly going to set me free?"

Cailleach nodded, but I could almost feel the catch coming before she opened her mouth. "Ye can make love to one woman only until her life ends; the others will turn into dragons, to remind ye of the beast ye were to Brìghde. Choose wisely. One woman is all you'll get. Then I know ye won't use her and cast her aside."

Kerdik's mouth fell open in time with mine and Lane's. He cleared the space between us, feeling around for me and then jerking me to his chest. He laid one on me that was passionate enough to make my knees buckle. Too many emotions flooded through me – relief, longing and finally, chagrin. It happened so fast that I didn't have the wherewithal to protest. His hunger for me was heady, and I felt powerless to sort out any kind of higher brain function.

Worse than that, I didn't want to stop him. I wanted more, and still more.

So I took what didn't belong to me yet, and what might always be mine. I took Kerdik's affections and locked them tight in my heart, swooning for the love that was always bigger than I could wrap my mind around.

When my morals finally caught up with my libido, I gently extracted myself from the kiss I hadn't meant to land myself in. I stumbled back, touching my forehead in concern as I whirled to face Cailleach. "But I'm engaged to Bastien! You know that, and you're still limiting him like this?"

Cailleach's snark mutated to a full-blown smile. "He doesn't have to choose ye."

"Rosie. I want only Rosie." His gaze was firm as it locked in on mine. "I can wait for you. I don't care how long it takes."

I ignored Lane's moan of frustration when I moved forward to land myself in Kerdik's arms. I kept my head on straight this time, and didn't kiss him. "I'll understand if you can't wait. I want you to be happy."

"I know, but I'll always and only want you."

"Very well, then." Cailleach reached her hand out and touched Kerdik's elbow, sending a chill through him that had a spark of magic to it. His body seemed to pulse against mine, alerting me to the fact that I was a woman, and immortal though he was, Kerdik was very much a man.

His arms tightened around me as his lips found my forehead. The weather swirled, making my body tremble against his. Though he was shirtless, he covered me, as if I was the one who needed the shelter from the storm. His lips pressed to my ear and whispered a breathless, "I will give you as many green children as you want. Say the word, and I will come for you."

The kiss I gave him was my choice. It was only one kiss, but it was tender, laced with promises and assurances for the future. Then I pressed my cheek to his chest as my hand searched for his heart.

I could always find Kerdik's heart, though many swore it didn't exist.

Brìghde cried out, begging Kerdik for help, since her sister wanted nothing to do with wrangling up the dark magic. Kerdik cast me one more look of longing before he stumbled to Brìghde's side, recalling where his focus should be.

"Alright, then." Cailleach turned to me and gripped my chin hard. "Ye risked much by summoning me. Thank ye for saving my Brìghde."

I nodded, and then melted into her, hugging the blue-haired woman who tugged at my heartstrings and still had the hutzpah to make me furious on a dime. "Thank you for helping me. And thank you for setting Kerdik free."

Cailleach chuckled as she patted my back. "If you're still thanking me after fifty years of Kerdik's affections, then I'll know I made the right call." She pulled back and lifted my hand to thumb at my ring. She closed her eyes and murmured something that was lost in the howling wind. I gasped when the stone turned green as it heated up, and then when she released it, it cooled and faded back to its usual light blue. "See tha this ring stays on your finger."

21

FIGHTING FOR FAÎTE

Kerdik grumbled, looking over his shoulder at Cailleach and me. "I already put my protection on her. You didn't need to do that. I can look after what's mine."

"None of this matters! Focus on the lost magic, Kerdik!" I shouted, reminding him of the greater problems we'd been ignoring to regroup. "That's the only thing we should be working on!"

Cailleach didn't pay attention to Kerdik and her sister, but turned to Lane. "Did ye help free my sister?"

"I was of less help than I wanted to be, but yes, that was the plan."

Cailleach nodded, and then palmed her face. Lane screamed, but the terror lasted the span of two seconds. When Cailleach pulled her hand away, Lane's lacerations were repaired, leaving a long, shiny, pink line to remind the world of this harrowing day.

The ice wall crumbled, revealing Bastien surrounded by yet more dead bodies. His chest heaved as he blinked at us, the bloodlust clear in his eyes.

"Untouchable," Cailleach said, moving toward him. "Ye helped to save my Brìghde, too. What is it ye wish from me as a gift of my gratitude?"

Bastien was stunned, looking from Cailleach to my face with shrugged shoulders. "I'm just glad it all worked out. Thanks for the cloaks, and the help getting over here."

Cailleach eyed him, walked over, reached up and gripped his collar. She yanked him down and pressed her thin lips to his, kissing the crap out of my fiancé, who was wide-eyed as his arms flailed out to the sides. I'm sure I should've said something, but the sight was so strange, I couldn't find a single word. To me, she was a smoking hot woman kissing my dude, but to Bastien, an old hag was laying one on him. It was actually pretty funny.

When she released him, she patted his cheek with a snigger. "My gift will come in handy when you're in need."

Bastien patted his chest, as if to feel where she'd snuck him an extra canteen or something. "Thank you, your majesty."

"No, no. Thank *you*. It's been a while since I kissed a warrior." Then the blue-haired woman walked out to the balcony and wrapped her arm around Brìghde. "Come, now. It's time to go home. Kerdik can clean up the mess."

"No, he can't! He's kept the higher magic hidden for far too long. It's our turn to help!"

Cailleach's jaw tightened. "At what cost to ye?"

Wild rage welled up in Brìghde, and then spewed onto her sister. "At any cost! I'll not see Faîte so twisted by the darkness. This is our world, Callie! Ye forget your role, sister. Without us, they have no one! If we leave them to whither under the higher magic, we're no better than Carman and the Brothers of Destruction!"

Cailleach's nostrils flared with anger, but with a labored sigh, finally added her weight to the mix. She stretched out her hand and seemed to grab at the purple streaks, yanking them back and whipping them across the sky to gather up the rest like a lasso. So many threads were still escaping, but an immortal at full strength was exactly the cavalry we needed. "Rosie!" she called, and then jerked her chin for me to come out into the storm next to Kerdik. "Give me your hand!"

I extended my right hand to her, trembling as it was. She smacked my palm down on the balcony, ignoring my wince from the torrential weather that whipped at me. I shrieked as the purple and black began to jerk toward us. Callieach pulled the strands harder, straining against the invisible bucking bronco that didn't want to be tamed any longer.

I screamed when the black tentacle touched my ring. It burned as the fog started to recede back into the prison it had been trapped in since before I'd come to Avalon.

Bastien and Lane were at my sides in the next breath, holding me upright and making sure my hand didn't move through the agony that rippled through my body. On and on the torrents of searing agony went, making me lose my grip on toughing it out as a scream ripped from my throat. So many things were compounding to tear the fury from me. Too many months of fighting to keep Avalon from splintering apart finally built into an explosion of agony I'd been pretending I didn't feel, couldn't see and didn't understand.

But I understood every ounce of Avalon's agony, for it had become my own.

Just when I thought I couldn't take another second, the tail of the black and purple mass vanished into my ring. The burning finally stopped, leaving me breathless. I sagged against Lane and Bastien, letting them support me as my knees buckled and my head flopped back.

"There's still more!" Brìghde nearly fell under the weight of too much that life was expecting from her. "The higher magic is airborne! It might travel to our land. I don't want that for our people!"

Cailleach caught her sister before Brìghde fell. "Brìghde has done all she can, and she'll not be expected to do more. I've trapped most of the lost magic; Kerdik can do the rest."

"No, Callie!" Brìghde's protest sounded drunken and slurred.

Kerdik's voice was calm. "I'll do all I can," he assured

them. "Go to Éireland and reinforce your wards. The darkness is coming, and as much as Avalon will be infected, it will find its way home to your land."

Cailleach nodded, taking Kerdik's warning seriously. "We will. Good luck, Kerdik."

Then the two sisters vanished from Avalon, leaving us to the mess.

22

THE DARKNESS INSIDE OF ME

"I waited too long," Kerdik said as he glared at the sky. His arms were raised to the forbidding clouds as if he was conducting an orchestra. "Cailleach distracted me by drawing out talk of my curse. Too much higher magic is tumbling through the sky now. I'll never be able to get it all back! There's all these little threads I can't quite grip."

I stood at Kerdik's side on the edge of the balcony, grateful that the sleet, snow, rain and hail had come to a halt. Now it was just the wind that whipped at us, chilling me to the bone. "What can I do to help?"

Kerdik shot me a quick smirk. "Just stand here by my side." He moved my hand from Bastien's and placed it back on the stone railing of the balcony, not bothering to address Bastien at all in the exchange. "Hold your hand here again, darling. Whatever you do, keep your ring still.

It might get hot again when I put more of the darkness back inside."

"This is still the plan? Are you sure that's such a great idea? I mean, if Morgan found a way around it, someone else will soon enough."

"But you'll be in Common with your husband. No one from Avalon will venture there." He shot me a firm look that told me he was dealing with the inevitable. "Either the darkness goes into this ring, or it goes into Faîte. Your choice."

I closed my eyes and nodded. "Alright. Do it to it."

Kerdik moved to make space for Lane, and motioned her to stand on my other side. "You two will need to make sure her hand stays still. If Cailleach said not to take off the ring, under no circumstances will she take it off for the rest of her life. Understood?"

Bastien and I both nodded with the grave acceptance of all we were being entrusted to watch over.

"Very well. Brace yourselves now. This is going to hurt." Kerdik turned to the sky, his jaw tight.

I kept my whimpering to an internal bleat, to save Kerdik from any guilt that might dissuade him from making the right call for Avalon. Bastien was on my right and Lane was on my left. Each of them put an arm around my back to brace me, and secured my wrist to the balcony to keep me in place. Lane nodded to Kerdik. "Alright. We've got her."

Kerdik closed his eyes and gripped the balcony, leaning

on it and hunching his shoulders as he geared up for some major magic wrangling. There were no spells that spilled from his lips, but when he raised his hands to the massive swirling cloud overhead, we all braced for the blow. Brighde had set the sky in motion, and left the dark clouds whirling in the air like a spinning top. The tiny threads of black and purple began to inch together, squeaking toward the center of the vortex. Kerdik let out a cry, and the tiny snakes began to dip down, like taffy being pulled toward us. I inhaled sharply when the snakes neared, and the invisible tether was coerced into my ring.

The sting was minimal, but surprised me nonetheless. The second the magic realized it was being trapped by my ring, it began to revolt, tugging against Kerdik's command.

Kerdik's hands remained raised, not caring what freedom the higher magic wanted. He mimed yanking an invisible force toward us with a sharp grunt, and more of the snakes filtered into my ring, turning the sting up to a sharp slice. I gasped, but didn't pull away, staring with fascination at what felt like a knife across my ring finger, but left not a single mark.

Kerdik wrestled with the defiant strings in the sky as if arguing with a teenager. Though the lost magic wanted to infect the world with its rage against the machine, Kerdik was in charge, and he wasn't about to be bested by the rebellion. I gritted my teeth through the phantom blade across my finger, closing my eyes as the pain ramped up and started heating. It wasn't until Lane shouted, "Rosie, stay still!" that I realized I was twitching and trying to wriggle away from the scald.

"I'm trying! It's burning my hand!" I threw my head back and let my knees buckle when the heat traveled through my arm like a full-on fire that bled into the rest of my body. The snakes were fighting with me now, trying to make me see reason as if I had a say in any of it.

Through it all I kept my hand in place, doing my best to endure so I could be a team player. It wasn't until two different black spindles broke off from the fog and tickled my nose that I lost my shiz. I thrashed while Bastien tried to keep me in place, hold my arm steady, and cover my nose to keep the bad things away. "Kerdik!" I screamed. My opened mouth was all the black snakes were waiting for. The two slipped into my mouth and wriggled down my throat, tormenting my insides.

Bastien's roar was the only thing I heard. "Kerdik, help! Something went into her mouth!"

"If I stop now, the rest of the darkness will go into Avalon. I'll help her once I'm finished."

The cloud seemed triumphant in its victory of sneaking inside of me. The snakes were slithering around, bumping into my DNA and changing things they weren't supposed to be touching. I screamed as something popped in my mouth, cutting my gums like a million knives doing surgery on whatever the crap they felt like.

Of all the things to feel in the middle of a battle on the nebulous, hunger hit my belly, coiling with desperation I couldn't ignore. I went from my sole focus being the pain, to a ravenous hunger being the only thing in my life. I don't know when the last time was that I'd eaten, but I knew I couldn't last another minute, starving as I was. The number of snakes in the sky were getting smaller, sucking into my ring while Kerdik called out commands I couldn't decipher. I could hear the anxiety in his voice, but the hunger was more powerful than even that. My head twisted left and right, searching for something to fill my belly. I couldn't remember my appetite ever being this voracious, and felt the urge to murder anyone who got in the way of me and my Happy Meal.

Lane was freaking out about something, but I couldn't understand her words. Of all the chaos that surrounded me, my ears suddenly went deaf to all sounds, except a steady thrumming that sounded like the relief I needed and the man I craved. The anarchy of the world I was stuck in began to fade, the pandemonium submitting to the tune of the kettle drum that centered my focus and made my mouth water.

Bastien smelled like cinnamon, and I wanted to be nearer to the scent that tempted me. He leaned in, cradling me to his chest as he studied my features with a wrinkled brow. He was shouting something to Kerdik, but all I heard was that beautiful thumping that seemed to stir something delicious inside of me. I didn't feel the pain of my finger anymore, or the slices in my mouth, nor the fear of something foreign swirling around inside my body. All I felt was the draw of the steady beat that called to me like a forbidden lover.

Only Bastien wasn't forbidden. He'd said a million times that what was his was as good as mine. He was all mine for the taking.

So I took him. On instinct I didn't have the where-withal to comprehend, I opened my mouth and latched my lips onto Bastien's neck, sucking at the pulse that teased my baser senses.

Bastien's lashes fluttered in the midst of the bedlam. "Oh, holy... Rosie, not now!"

When sucking and licking his skin didn't suffice, my stomach roared that I wanted more. I didn't think, only acted on a pure animal instinct that made no sense to my brain. I bit down on my fiancé's neck, piercing his skin and drinking his warmth into my mouth.

The succulent treat that flowed down my throat was like nothing I'd ever tasted before. It was beyond a flavor classification, but had the scent of cinnamon and Bastien to it. I heard Lane scream as my arm pushed her aside when she tried to jerk me away. I didn't care about being still for the cloud; I only cared that Bastien stayed put, so I could feast on him to my heart's content. I pushed him over with strength I didn't know I had, jerking his head to the side so I could take what I needed. My eyes fluttered shut as my body writhed with a slow, luscious, sensual persuasion atop his struggling form. I heard myself groan like a porn star – guttural and forceful. Everything in me needed Bastien. I was starved for him, and couldn't hold back.

Kerdik wrestled me off my prey, shouting things I didn't care to hear. I lunged time after time, but he fought with me until I twisted to bite my green captor, using my new weapon with an instinct I was too rabid to comprehend.

Kerdik didn't howl, but he did grimace at the small bite marks I left on his wrist before he shook me off.

An acrid taste flooded my mouth, pushing out the cinnamon deliciousness. I spat the foreign grossness out on the balcony. "Ack! Sick! You taste disgusting!"

Kerdik straightened, looking down his nose at me. It was as if I'd said something he was willing himself not to hold me accountable for. "That'll be the last time you say that to me."

I turned toward Bastien, who was backed to the railing of the balcony, pale and in shock as he gaped at me. His hand was over his bleeding neck, covering the treasure I craved. I took a step toward him, but Kerdik's arms around me held me tight to his chest, my back pressed to his front. "Let me go! I need him!"

"Easy, darling. There's something inside of you that I need to draw out. You don't want to hurt him, do you?"

"Of course not. I would never hurt Bastien."

"You just attacked him!" Lane screeched. "Kerdik, tell me she's not... Tell me my baby's not a Vampire!"

The obvious word punched into me like a Mike Tyson-sized dose of non-reality. My gaze jerked back to Bastien, who looked horrified and frightened. Bastien was never afraid. Now I could see it all clearly on his face.

Bastien was scared of me.

I didn't want to lunge, but my body ached for the blood it had been denied. Kerdik wrestled me to the floor, rolling me over so he could peer into my mouth. "Lane, help me hold her still! I have to get it out before it sets down roots."

Lane moved around to my legs, pinning them down as tears flowed from her face. "It's alright, baby. It'll be fine. Kerdik can fix you."

"I need Bastien!" I screamed, not caring that I sounded like a codependent twit. I needed more of that cinnamon sweetness in my mouth. My body was twitching for him, pushing me to do whatever it took to get another hit, and another.

Kerdik cupped his hand over my mouth, gripping my face sideways. "*Manifester*!" he called to whatever it was inside of me that he wanted to come out.

The snakes trapped in my body jerked around, burrowing deeper to escape Kerdik's command. Again, he said it, and again, until the magnetic pull he possessed tugged them into his hand. The ends broke off, but the bulk of the madness was finally in his grip. Both black threads were jerked out of me, like a magician pulling a bunch of bananas from a volunteer in the audience. The snakes writhed in his fist until he released them over my ring. The aquamarine trapped them inside so they couldn't torment me anymore.

Kerdik slumped over my supine form in relief. "I got them both. She'll be alright."

"Then why do her teeth still look like that?" Lane demanded, furious and fearful.

Kerdik propped himself up on his elbows to peer into my mouth. What reprieve the vanishing snakes had given him was now gone. "No. No, no. No. I can fix this." Though his tone had the desperation of a man who was grasping at straws, I tried to trust him. He covered my mouth again and shouted, "*Manifester!*" again, but nothing inside of me moved. The broken-off bits of darkness were seeping into my bones now, taking root and melting into my innermost parts.

I'd felt things shift inside of me when the higher magic had first entered, and knew something was different. Though I could hear now through my fog of wanting more blood, the desire was still coursing through me.

"Kerdik?" I whispered, my lower lip trembling. "What's wrong with me?"

Kerdik let out a cry of frustration, reaching between us to feel along my rib cage. He moved off of me and tore my shirt up, paying my noise of surprise no mind as he pressed his ear to my stomach, as if his hearing had all the powers of an ultrasound.

I meant to open my mouth and ask more politely if I could please, please, please have just a little more blood, but when I tried, a horrible wail came from my lips.

"More!" I cried, scared at how distressed my voice sounded.

Kerdik swore and covered my mouth again. "It's in there. In deep, Lane. I can't get it out! There's no undoing it now. We just have to wait to see if she's a *Farouche* or an *Attelage*."

Lane was beside herself, her voice dripping with grief. "My daughter's not a Vampire!"

Kerdik snarled at her. "You think I don't wish there was any other explanation?" The fear in his eyes scared me more than my need for blood. Kerdik was never afraid, so I knew this would be bad. "Darling," he said quietly, hovering above my horizontal form. "What's my name?"

I wanted to cry out for more blood, but knew that wasn't what he was asking me. "Kerdik," I panted. "Kerdik, something's wrong with me. I want to drink blood! I need it!"

Kerdik exhaled with choked relief. He turned his chin up to look at Lane. "Be grateful she isn't a *Farouche*. We don't have to figure out how to put her down. She can learn to live with this."

"Bastien!" I cried out, partly because I needed more of his blood, but also because I was scared that something was changing, and I didn't understand what.

Kerdik sat back, motioning for Lane to release my legs. I had the freedom to attack Bastien if I wanted to, but this time I was more measured in my hunger. I knew if I pounced, they'd take me away from him. Animal that I was, I needed sustenance.

Shooting furtive glances at Kerdik to see how much tether he'd give me, I crawled over to my fiancé, whose hand was dripping with the food my stomach was screaming to get at. Still, I paced myself, taking in Bastien's sweaty face and pale pallor. I knew I couldn't drain him anymore, but oh, how I wanted to.

"Bastien?"

His reply came back breathy and unsteady. "It's alright, Daisy. I'm okay. Are you feeling better?"

I didn't know how to answer that, so I didn't. Despite our audience, I climbed onto his lap, straddling his thighs so I could wrap my arms around Bastien to comfort him. The blood called out to me, singing my name like a vixen. I reasoned that if it was dripping all over him just going to waste, it wouldn't put him in peril to clean him up a bit. I pried his hand from his neck, feeling Kerdik standing over us, ready to intervene. "Please," I begged quietly with longing in my eyes. "I won't bite. Just a taste."

Bastien looked up to Kerdik to see what he should do, and then nodded, turning his head away so he didn't have to see me lick the blood off his hands and run my tongue along the strained ridges of his neck.

23

MY NEW VAMPY LIFE

The trip home was solemn, and made without me. When Kerdik insisted I be kept away from the others, no one argued, though I could tell Bastien wanted to. Bastien refused to leave me in Province 1, but Kerdik was firm that we stay away from each other for two full days. "You'll drink too much blood. You need to learn what it feels like to abstain, or you'll seriously hurt him."

You would've thought Kerdik had forcefully ripped Romeo away from his Juliet, what with the way the two of us carried on. I'm not sure what my deal was, but Bastien was just as belligerent. "If she needs my blood, then she can have it. Why am I suddenly not allowed to live with my charge? Why is it a good idea to send her off with you?"

Kerdik had rolled his eyes at our dramatics. I'd been weeping – actually weeping – in Bastien's arms. After all we'd been through, I'd be willing to punch anyone square in the face for judging me.

Kerdik sighed. "You're nervous to leave her because you're bonded even more so now. You've got her *lueur*, and on top of that you're her mate – the only one she can drink blood from. The bond between an *Attelage* Vampire and her mate? It's intense, and you two are already on my last nerve. Add being engaged to that? Everything you're feeling is normal, but you need to get a grip on it. Two days apart is necessary for her to realize she can go that long without blood, and for you to understand that she's allowed to be in a different building without you having a heart attack. You'll smother her with the angst I can already see rising up inside of you at the mere mention of being apart for two short days."

It took another half an hour of arguing between the two bulls, but ultimately Bastien gave in when Kerdik lured him away with work related to keeping me safe. He was commissioned to round up two dozen of Morgan's soldiers and take them out to draw out the *Farouche* Vampires, locking them in Morgan's dungeon before they could hurt more people. Kerdik was clear that the problem needed to be dealt with immediately, and Bastien was just insane enough to go on a Vampire hunt.

So Bastien was allowed to stay in Province 1, but he spent his time rounding up the *Farouche* Vampires, not permitted into the castle until two full days passed. Kerdik kept a vial of Bastien's blood in his pocket, just in case.

Apparently, I wasn't supposed to need so much after that first gluttonous gorging I'd done.

Though Kerdik's reasoning was solid, my mouth watered every time anyone said Bastien's name. Kerdik and I tried to distract ourselves from my altered genetics and did what we could to clean up Province 1. The remaining soldiers, jaded and somewhat entitled as they were, defaulted to my rule since I was the daughter of their fallen leader. Still, Kerdik kept a close eye on me to make sure none of them misbehaved.

"You're too soft on the soldiers," Kerdik observed. "They can dig faster than that, and you don't need to help them." The romance between us had been tucked away, both of us respecting that I was engaged for as long as it was until Bastien decided I was too much to handle with my Vampiric qualities, and tossed me to the curb. Kerdik and I were friends now, which put one less complication on my plate.

I didn't put down my shovel, but paused the digging that Kerdik had argued up and down wasn't my job to do. "I'm not above working to make Avalon better. What's it to you if I help rebuild a broken country?"

"Because your rebuilding should be done from the throne."

I scoffed, not bothering to lower my voice. "Please. These guys don't want me on the throne any more than I want to be there. They've been through enough."

Kerdik glared at each of the five dozen men, who all

shoveled with their heads lowered, lest they make eye contact with the almighty Master Kerdik and incur his wrath. "They've *put* Avalon through enough, you mean. These are the men who rape and pillage, Rosie. Morgan's soldiers followed her without question."

"Then they understand loyalty," I snapped, cutting him off. "That's a good quality, and if it's the only worthwhile attribute they've got, I won't stamp it out." I cast around furtively at the men who were all bigger and stronger than me. "But the raping and the pillaging will catch them a swift death. You heard it here first, guys. Your new job is to make Avalon safer for the civilians. So after we bury all these bodies, you're going to start planting crops for the people you wronged." When I heard a murmuring in the ranks, I held up my hand. "Fight me on this, and I'll take my mother's throne so fast, you won't know what hit you. Then your full-time jobs will be to sing me songs and paint me pictures of unicorns and flowers. Fix what you broke, you jags." I launched the edge of my shovel into the dirt, picking my rhythm back up of scooping and dumping. "I get that you don't feel you had a choice in any of it, but if you can follow Morgan's orders to be demanding buttholes, you can sure as a kick in the teeth follow my request to make the world a better place."

"You should be on the throne," Kerdik grumbled through gritted teeth.

I rubbed out a kink in my neck. "I addressed what's left of Province I this morning. I did the royalty thing. Now I'm doing the citizen thing. Taking care of Avalon is what I'm supposed to be doing. Right now, this is what Avalon needs. They need a ruler who gives a crap about them. Dead bodies left out for anyone to see? I care about them, and they need to see that. Maybe if they do, they'll remember again what made this land great."

Kerdik's hat that he'd given me long ago had been returned to him. He'd worn it all morning before placing the Newsies cap on my head to shield my eyes from the sun. It was sweet, but he still maintained a polite distance, keeping an eye on me while standing back so we didn't complicate our lives any further. "What a sweet world you live in."

"Yes. Well, if you're lucky, you just might get invited to the party once we get things up and running."

"They're going to turn on you the second you're alone, you know." Kerdik didn't bother lowering his voice, letting his observation carry through the ranks.

"Really? I'm not prom queen yet? Total bummer. What's a girl with a plucky can-do smile and a shovel gotta do to win over the rapists?"

Okay, maybe my attitude was a little over the top, but you try working with glorified criminals when all you want is more blood in your tummy, and see how cool you play it. I was sweating in the humid and balmy climate, the sun making my once-white t-shirt stick to my back.

A soldier named Maurice spoke up from behind me. "Not all of us took advantage of our status. Some of us did as we were ordered and then went home to our families."

Kerdik's tone was sharp before I could get out a single world. "You dare address the Avalon Rose without kneeling? She may not care about her title, but I'll see that it's honored."

Maurice fell to his knees, his chin lowered. "Forgive me for my candor, your majesty most high."

I stuck my shovel in the ground and took off my hat to wipe the sweat from my brow. "Oh, jeez. You don't have to call me that. Kerdik's just in a mood. K, can you think of a title that doesn't sound so pretentious? I don't mind them calling me just plain old Ro, but something tells me you might have a problem with that. Can you think of a title that's somewhere in between?"

"How about, 'Rosalie, most powerful'?" Kerdik suggested.

"Pass. We're going for *not* pretentious, here."

Kerdik touched his chin in thought. "Queen Rosalie of Avalon isn't strong enough."

I rolled my eyes. "Oh, forget it. I'll just be the Lost Daughter of Avalon."

Maurice kept his head bowed. "If I may, your grace. How about, "Rosalie, the Gentle?"

A sweetness fell over me, endearing me to the nickname. "Aw, I think I might like that one. It'll make me try harder to live up to the hype. Good job, dude. Rosie the Gentle it is, then. You can get up now; Kerdik doesn't bite."

I winced at my phrasing. Kerdik didn't bite, but I sure did. I'd been half a day without Bastien's blood, and though I didn't feel like tearing into any of the guys, I wasn't as clearheaded as I wanted to be. Too much turmoil roiled around inside my gut. My mother was dead, and the worst part was that the news of that tragedy was supposed to be a good thing. I'd murdered a woman, which felt like a giant step back for feminism or humanity, or something. I had a new desire to suck down my boyfriend's blood, so much that he'd had to leave until I got ahold of myself. Top that all off with him having my *lueur* inside of him still, and I felt supremely unbalanced.

There was also the wake of vultures, who were swooping in to pick at the bodies we couldn't move fast enough to bury. I could hear them chattering to each other as they ate, making me blanch that they actually knew some of the correct names of the body parts.

Then there was the matter of the surviving soldiers, who I didn't bother trying to pretend I could trust. I think the part of me that believed the best in people was starting to die off. After all I'd been through, that felt like the lowest note somehow.

I went back to digging. Though we'd been at it all morning and it was passing lunchtime, I didn't stop. The mass grave needed to be big enough to fit all the bodies that had fallen in the massacre.

When Rigby came out to get us, Kerdik stepped closer to me. I didn't totally understand my reasons for letting

Rigby live, but it didn't feel right offing someone who had been so obviously controlled. I'd told Kerdik that Rigby's head belonged to Brighde, who could take her revenge on him for his espionage whenever she wished. Since his temporary pardon, Rigby had been the perfect number two, as he'd been trained so thoroughly to be for Morgan. "Your grace, your lunch is ready."

I kept my eyes on the shovel. "Oh, that's alright. I'm not hungry. You can have my lunch. It shouldn't go to waste."

Rigby's shoulders remained tight, his posture perfect. "If you're not hungry now, when shall I tell Fabien you'll be dining?"

I shrugged. "Maybe I'll catch you all for dinner."

Kerdik and Rigby shook their heads as if they were tied to the same string, but Kerdik was the only one who over-ruled me. Rigs was too diplomatic for that. "You'll take a break now. The soldiers aren't allowed to break for a meal if you've ordered them to work, and not everyone is as into self-flagellation as you are." Kerdik's voice was clipped when he addressed the sweaty men. "You'll take your lunch now and return to dig the grave of your fellow man when you've washed and finished eating. Nature is my spy, so the rocks and trees will inform me if there's any treachery brewing in the ranks." He looked to the sun that blazed, when just yesterday we'd been caught up in a bliz-zard. "Province 1 has only a single jewel left, which is more than enough to sustain the people here. However, it may take some adjusting to get used to the hotter climate.

Drink water. I fear I have no patience for your weariness today. When you've finished with your break, dig the rest of this grave in silence. Then you'll fill it in with the bodies of the fallen. Rosie the Gentle will have her lunch now."

I scowled up at Kerdik as the soldiers put down their shovels and stretched. "Master Kerdik, oh wise one, thank you for bossing me and telling me when I'm hungry. I'm just a simple girl, and need a big, strong man like yourself to let me know when I should eat."

Kerdik was familiar with my sass when I was separated from my *lueur*. He cast me a cocky look with a little swagger mixed in. "Always call me 'Master Kerdik, oh wise one,' and 'big, strong man.' Into the castle with you."

I grumbled and made no move to obey. I kept on shoveling, ignoring the wary looks from the soldiers. They were more than happy to take a break and escape Kerdik's temper, which swung with all the grace of a wrecking ball.

"What are you murmuring?" Kerdik asked, his tone sharp.

"I said, 'bite me.' You see those huge birds over there? That one with the broken tailfeathers sent a message to his buddy to bring more vultures in from the forest to tell them about the feast. None of you may care about the people getting scavenged over, but I do." I held up my hand to stave off Kerdik's protest. "I'm not asking you to be all compassionate toward the people who called for more beatings when you were tied up. I'm just telling you that I care, so let me."

"You're impossible."

"You're dreamy," I simpered. "Did anyone ever tell you that you're an absolute love bug?"

"Get out of the pit."

"What? No. I just said I wasn't finished."

"I was only letting you do this because you seem to need to do something with your hands when your life tips on its head. You didn't go to sleep at all last night. You're exhausted, and getting on my last nerve."

"I feel like I already told you to bite me. Did you need me to say it again?"

Rigby intervened before Kerdik and I could devolve further into our childishness. The soldiers had already vacated the pit and were scurrying away from Kerdik. Rigs remained on the edge of the mass grave, peering down at me. "Your grace, the servants were wondering where you'd like your things moved."

"My things?"

"Your mother's things, which are now yours. Where would you like them? I can have the servants box them up for you so you can take the queen's bedroom, if you like."

I hadn't thought about any of the estate stuff that happened when your parent died. "Oh, um, I'm not sure. Maybe I should go give it a look and see what's what."

Rigby kept his chin lowered to me at all times, even as he extended his elbow to me. "Splendid idea, your grace. I'll see to having lunch sent to your new bedroom so you can eat while you work, if that's your wish."

I sighed. "Okay, yeah. Thanks, Rigs."

Rigby's neck stiffened, finally bringing himself to look at my face with a stern expression. "No. You'll not forgive me for my transgressions. I do not deserve the name you gave me when I held your trust. I have my head, which is more than I expected to keep. I'll not take your kindness, as well. Save your grace for those who deserve it."

With that, Rigby went ahead of us into the castle, tending to the house so he didn't have to look me in the eye anymore.

24

MY NEW DIGS, AND GOOD OLD RIGS

Kerdik watched the dynamic between Rigby and me without taking over, which was huge progress for him. He extended his elbow to me even though I was filthy, mud spattering my jeans and tank top. Despite our squabbling, I was grateful Kerdik stayed with me, monster though I was now. "I'm sorry," I whispered. "I know I'm being a pill today."

"Yes, you are. But I know you. I know you're picking a fight to avoid talking about it all."

"Does that mean we can have the whole the-truth-is-out-there speech another time?"

"I'm afraid you need to know what's happened to you so you don't accidentally murder Bastien. Though, that would save me decades of loneliness, so really, you can remain in the dark as long as you like."

I sighed as we walked over the bridge, past two guards

and into the castle that felt like a mausoleum to me. That was the other reason I was avoiding sleep. I didn't want to see the place that held such bitter memories. I stayed tight to Kerdik, my eyes falling on the nine remaining household servants. They were all lined up for me in the foyer, like I was supposed to give them some kind of Captain Von Trapp inspection or something. "Um, hey everyone. What's up?"

Kerdik sighed at my lack of royal training. "This is what's left of your staff after the massacre. The others who survived but proved disloyal to you were executed while you were digging your precious hole."

I gasped. "You didn't have to do that!" I accused with a scowl of indignation.

"It's no trouble." He turned to the staff. "The Lost Daughter of Avalon's new title shall be 'Rosie the Gentle.' See that you adhere to it. While she may be tender, I am not, and will happily see to it she's treated like the queen you should fear."

I rolled my eyes. "Jeez, Kerdik. This is awkward enough."

His posture was stiff and commanding, his jaw tight as he surveyed the servants, who all looked ready to pee themselves. "I don't care. You're my queen, and you'll be respected as such."

I slowly turned my chin up to gaze at him, understanding finally that this was how he looked out for me. It was how he saw his role when we eventually would become a family. I wasn't sure what to do with that, so I simply held onto his arm and leaned my temple to his shoulder to soften his rigid demeanor.

Rigby went down the line, introducing me to everyone, who I mostly remembered. When we got to the end, Fabien the chef bowed his head to me. "Forgive me, your grace, but I'm not sure what to cook for you. I know you don't eat meat, but with your new... enhancements, I don't know what else you require."

Kerdik answered for me. "She's an *Attelage* Vampire, not a *Farouche*. She consumes regular food, and is bound to her fiancé, Bastian the Bold. You needn't worry about procuring blood for her, though I do appreciate the attention to detail."

"Welcome back, your grace." Fabien met my eyes with that hint of sweetness I remembered when I'd hidden in the kitchen long ago. His forearms were massive, but his meek demeanor made him look absolutely precious. "The castle was most empty without you here."

I softened at his sweetness. "Thanks, man. I missed you, too."

Fabien bowed, and Kerdik escorted me to my old bedroom, ordering for a *soumettre* to draw me a bath and fetch me clean clothes (his words, not mine).

When I stood in the doorway of my old room, too many memories came back to me – both good and bad. My eyes fell on the posts of my bed, where I'd braced myself while Demi had tightened my corset beyond what the Surgeon General would've allowed. There was the window where I had chatted with any number of birds to keep myself company when I'd been locked inside. Then there was the bed on the raised platform, looking like a statement of sex and opulence rather than a piece of furniture.

I gulped as I pictured Demi lounging on my mattress, us rubbing each other's feet and laughing together while we traded stories and sweet kisses. I knew he was a slave used for sex, but our relationship had been so innocent. Lately, none of my life felt young and naïve anymore. I wondered how much of my youth had been murdered when Demi lost his head.

I took a step back, afraid to get too close to the pain. "I... Is it okay if I crash somewhere else? A couch somewhere or the floor in a different room. This isn't... I can't..."

Rigby understood. "Of course, your grace. Shall I take you to your mother's chambers so you can sort through her things? I can draw you a bath in there."

I nodded. "I guess that would be better than this." I kept my chin low, not making eye contact as I spoke to Rigs over my shoulder. "Did Demi's family ever get his things?"

"No, your grace. *Soumettres* don't have possessions. We *are* possessions, belonging to the queen."

I blanched. "Did Demi have anything he liked that his family might want?"

"From what I understand his family is quite poor. I'm sure anything, even his old clothes, would be appreciated.

They're in Province 10 now, though, so my guess is they're surviving better than they were here."

I nodded. "Clothes, then. And the book about Michel Fourniret. Demi loved that story. Would you mind boxing up a few outfits for his family?" I counted out his siblings, asking for clothes to be brought for each of them.

"As you wish it, your majesty." His eyes finally met mine as I stood in the doorway. There was a note of pleading in his gaze. Though he'd made it clear he didn't want forgiveness, I saw the brokenness that plagued him. "Anything you wish, please tell me."

25

VAMPIRE 101

Kerdik swept through the room, seeking out errant magic that might booby trap me if I stepped on the wrong stone or something. Rigby drew me a bath and went out to bring my lunch, leaving me with Kerdik.

"You'll be safe in here," Kerdik ruled, sniffing the heavy red drapes that stretched from floor to ceiling. "The servants who remain seem trustworthy, serving the throne no matter who's on it. They have no family anymore. If you want them, they can stay."

"Fine by me. I'm only going to be here until Dad can send over someone real to rule. So long as I don't get attacked, I'm cool. I've hit my limit on getting jumped, though, so spread it around for everyone to stop being a rapist, okay? I feel like that's just a good rule to follow in general."

"Of course." He pinched the bridge of his nose. "There are a few things I need to see to. I need to speak with Urien before the others reach him. I want to make sure my walls held through Morgan's soldiers' attack. I shouldn't be more than a day, but I really can't put it off much longer."

"It's cool. I'll be alright."

"I think Maurice can be trusted to guard you. If it's alright with you, I'll send word to have him posted outside your door until I return."

"Whatever works. Fine by me."

Kerdik sighed, and I could see the weariness in his soul that he only left exposed to me. "Get in the bath. I need to talk to you about everything, and I need you not to run out on the conversation."

I hung my head, knowing it was time for the grand Vampire talk. I moved behind the partition and peeled my sweaty and filthy clothes off, stepping into the golden tub with care. "Alright, hit me with it. I'm a monster villain now, right? Evil mustache, sharp fangs, luring young damsels into dark corners?"

"Hardly." He moved behind the partition to sit on the floor next to the tub, but I held my hands up to stop him, my fingers dripping over the edge.

"You have to talk to me from the other side of the partition. I'm engaged, Kerdik." I tried to be kind, but firm. When his brow creased in disapproval at being rebuffed, I held my ground. "When you and I are married someday, I don't think you'll want me to be naked around some other guy. Bastien deserves that same courtesy."

"Oh, fine." Kerdik rolled his eyes and moved to the other side, the division between us only a foot deep. "Can I at least picture you in the tub?"

"Probably not," I replied with a small smirk. We were no doubt having the same memory of the last time he'd sat with me while I was taking a bath in this castle, not too long ago in my bedroom just upstairs. Hopefully this bath wouldn't end in him losing his temper, and me being frozen in a block of ice.

Kerdik's voice was gentle. "Have I told you that I love you lately?"

I lathered up and started in on my toes, cleaning between each one. "You're stalling. You've been stalling all day. Just let the gavel drop. I drink blood now. I can go out in the sunlight, so that part's not true. My skin doesn't sparkle, either. Do I have to sleep in a coffin?"

I could picture Kerdik's nose crinkling. "What sort of education would lead you to those conclusions?"

"The television kind." I leaned my elbow on the lip of the opulent tub. I didn't have the guts to ask if the thing was real gold or not. Part of me didn't want the confirmation that people had been starving in other provinces while my mom had been bathing in a solid gold tub.

Kerdik let out a heavy sigh. "When the higher magic was set loose, Brìghde, Cailleach and I tried to wrangle it all, but some of it escaped. The element that went into you was Vampire. The *Attelage* kind." His tone shifted to an 'aw shucks' kind of sentiment. "I wish it had been a Banshee infection you'd caught. Those are nothing to be frightened of. Banshees merely have a deafening howl that comes when they sense a death is on its way that day. If the Dullahan suddenly rise up, the Banshee feel a kinship with them. That would have been so much easier than this."

"Who are the Dullahan?"

"The Headless Horsemen."

I stared ahead for a few seconds, my frown of disbelief unable to be stifled. "Oh, good. I was hoping you'd say something terrifying."

"They were extinct. All these creatures were. Some had absolutely terrible tempers."

That Kerdik thought someone had a foul temper worried me; his disposition was nothing to brag about. "I'm sure if I was headless, I'd be finicky, too."

"Now, about the Vampire curse." He drew in a deep breath, collecting his thoughts before exhaling. "There are two types of Vampires: the *Attelage* and the *Farouche*. The *Farouche* feed on anyone they can get their hands on. They have no conscience, no language, no desire other than blood, blood and more blood. When I go to Urien, no doubt hunting parties will be assembled to seek out the *Farouche* and destroy them."

"That's terrible! Is there an antidote or something that can help calm them down? You were able to draw out the black snake things from me. Can you do the same for them?"

Kerdik tapped his fingers along the partition, just to amuse himself with the sound of the light rhythm. "The *Farouche* are doomed. If you hadn't started talking and been able to reason, I would've had to lock you up, since you can't be killed by me."

"Grim, dude." I tried to picture Kerdik having to lock me away or figure out a way to end me. It was at that moment I decided whatever frustrations lie ahead with my new life, I would be grateful I hadn't ended up unsalvageable. "So I'm the *Attelage* kind, right? What does that mean?"

"It means that whoever you feed on first is the only one you'll feed on until your mate dies. Then you'll take a new mate, and it's the same thing." He paused a few beats. "Is the water tepid?"

"I don't mind."

"I'm coming back for only a minute." Kerdik popped his head behind the partition, smirking at my squinty eye that told him he was being a very naughty boy. He pressed a kiss to my naked shoulder as he stuck his finger into the water to warm it back up for me. My limbs loosened in the heat, and despite the conversation that made me want to bolt, I leaned my head back and paused washing myself just to relax for a few beats. Kerdik gazed into the water, and I knew he was wishing Rigby hadn't put so many bubbles in so he could see my body beneath the surface.

I lifted my finger out of the water and pointed back to the room. "Thank you, now over to the other side of the fake wall with you."

Kerdik narrowed his eyes at me, but acquiesced. "Bastien got to you first, which is just my luck, it seems. Had you fed on me first, it would be me you craved. Now everyone else's blood will be disgusting to you, and you and Bastien will only grow closer. Nothing comes between an *Attelage* and their mate."

"You don't want me to drink your blood. The whole thing's awful." The forbidden word made my tongue dry and my stomach growl. I fished around for the soap and ran my hand up my leg to scrub the day off of me.

"When Bastien passes on, you'll feed only from me." New light seemed to dawn on him. "The bond between a Vampire and their mate is unbreakable. When it's our time to be together, there will be no tearing us apart. And who knows what a daily dose of blood might do for your immortality. You might just get more than a double-portion of life." A sliver of optimism lightened his voice – the first glimmer of hope in too long. "That's a silver lining I can celebrate."

I laved water over my arms. "I don't understand why you're so good to me. I've been grouchy all day, and I'm engaged to someone else. Still, you act like I'm some special thing."

"You've always been my special thing."

I savored the words that made me feel precious, and then cleared my throat. "Tell me more about the monster I am now."

"Very well. An *Attelage* Vampire can live on a small dose of her mate's blood. I've seen some survive on as little as one meager teaspoon a week. But that was older Vampires with years of experience. You and Bastien will need to set up a schedule so you don't get too ravenous and attack him, as you did when you first drank. It's why I sent him away. You need to understand the hunger. Master it as much as you're able. He gave me enough of his blood to last you a week, if you limit yourself to one taste a day. Though he'll only be gone from you for two days, which you can manage."

I wanted to whine. I wanted to panic. I was so hungry for Bastien; I couldn't imagine lasting out the week like this. "I don't think I can make it that long!"

"You can, and it's important you do. Self-control, darling. If you want Bastien to live a long life with you, it behooves you not to drain every drop of blood from his body."

I pinched the bridge of my nose. "What are the other rules? What kills me? Like, silver stake to the heart? Do I flinch at crucifixes and the smell of garlic now?"

When Kerdik replied, his inflection sounded like he

thought I was a dummy. "I would imagine a silver stake to anyone's heart would do sufficient damage, but you can't be killed by anyone's hand, darling. You don't need to fear that. What else do you worry about? Tell me how I can fix it."

"I'm afraid I'll hurt Bastien."

"Well, that can happen. I've seen it plenty of times, especially during sex. Things get too heated, and the Vampire draws too much blood. A frenzy starts and the mate dies, usually either of heart failure or exsanguination. You won't have to worry about that with me when it's our time to be together, though. You can't kill me. I'll be able to give you everything you need."

I balked at him. "Well, lay it all out for me, why don't you? Did I just shorten Bastien's life by like, fifty years?"

Kerdik's reply was matter-of-fact. "I watched you. After the initial attack, you went back to being yourself. You asked for a taste, and you didn't bite him when you took it. And that was in the first hour of your change. Remarkable, really. You'll get the hang of it and learn the rhythm of your cravings so you don't attack him. You're used to denying yourself with your vegetarian diet. This is just another lesson in self-control you'll have no trouble mastering."

"You think so?"

"I know so. Be patient with the whole thing. Bastien knows enough about it all to make sure you don't get too hungry."

"But I'm hungry now," I admitted, guilt flickering in my eyes.

"I know, darling. And you'll learn to regulate yourself through the pain. You're the girl who stuck to her non-meat-eating ways even when you were being starved in that well. I have no doubt that you'll fare beautifully in this."

"How many days until I can eat again? I need to know what I'm dealing with. When is Bastien coming back?"

"Barely a day and a half. And your mother will be here just as soon as arrangements can be made for her province. I'll wrap this up as quick as a kingdom change can be done. While you wait, find ways to deal with the hunger so you know you can survive a few days without him, if necessary."

I bit my lip to chew on the new information as I scrubbed my back. So much had changed about me. "So I won't go attacking other people when I get hungry?"

"No. Do you want to drink my blood?"

I grimaced and dipped my hair into the water. "No, thanks."

Kerdik chuckled. "Other people's blood and even food will start to taste like sand in your mouth. The only thing you'll enjoy is Bastien's blood. You're a mild predator now, which means you're slightly more deadly in a fight, though not invincible," he warned.

"Okay, so that's the Vampire mojo. What did the second snake do?"

Kerdik stilled, his voice taut with apprehension. "What do you mean? I got them both out. It left its mark, sure, but you'll be able to control your urges well enough, since you weren't infected over a prolonged period of time."

"No, there were two. I saw two snakes go inside of me. Both had an end that broke off in my body before you yanked the bulk of them out."

Kerdik's eyes widened in horror. "Why didn't you say something? Come out of the tub right now!" He deflated with worry while I stepped out of the tub and wrapped the towel around me. "But it's been too long. It's set in you now. Rosie, no! What is it? What is it doing to you?"

I shrugged, perplexed as I came out from behind the partition. "I don't know. I mean, nothing so far, I don't think. Is there like, a monster glossary or something? I don't know what I'm supposed to be looking for."

Kerdik checked my spine, my palms, under both arms, my throat, my teeth, my tonsils, and finally my eyes. "I don't see anything else. That was really something you should've spoken up about."

I harrumphed. "One day I hope you come to Common just so you can try to keep up, and I can say condescending things like, 'You should really look both ways before you cross the street.'"

We stared at each other a few seconds, letting the weight of me traveling with some unknown bit of darkness rest between us. Kerdik's hands moved slowly around my waist, which was when I remembered I was still in a towel, and what we were doing was totally weird. I know, I'm slow on the uptake, but to be fair, I've now got a Vampire brain. "I'll get dressed."

Kerdik took in my dripping form and swallowed thickly. "I'll wait outside."

26

TEA TIME WITH RIGBY

Going through Morgan's stuff was a task I was unprepared for. Kerdik left me only after he'd sent for Maurice, and had given each of the soldiers and household staff members a talk that put untold fear in them and made them look at the floor whenever I came near. I sent Kerdik off with two barrels full of the crown jewels for Lane and my dad to keep in their treasury, and a modest fortune for Demi's family.

I took a break and spent a little time in the kitchen with Fabien. Fabien was huge and looked like he could do some serious damage with his massive fists, but he was meek as a kitten, working delicately with the pastry we rolled out together. He helped me make an apology gift for Bastien of a blackberry pie while I puzzled out what to do with Province 1 with Fabian. It was my traditional "I screwed up" offering – my very own humble pie.

Rigby and I were making decent progress with Morgan's bedroom after I'd taken care of a few points of business. It was your basic "Keep or Pitch" routine that had to be done. To my credit, I didn't cry once, and I only tripped over the hem of my gown six times. The long dress cut just below my breasts and hung loosely to the floor. I didn't mind the getup so much because I didn't have to wear a corset this time around. The long skirt was pink with gold trim, as were all my clothes when I lived here. The capped sleeves were pretty and delicate, reminding me that there were parts of me that weren't entirely monster. The birds that flew in and out of the bedroom window were gracious to my delicate state, and braided flowers in my hair when they sensed I was feeling low.

When the sun finally fell, my yawns couldn't be stifled. "Shall I summon a *soumettre* to warm your bed, your grace?" Rigby offered as he drew the curtains shut.

I blushed. "Oh, no thanks. I'm engaged to Bastien, so I'm not trying to be sleeping around. But if you could grab me some new sheets, I'd appreciate it. I don't feel right sleeping on hers."

"Of course, your majesty. No one has lain on them since my last rendezvous with Morgan, but if you wish it, new ones will be sent for."

I froze, not recalling until just then that not only had Rigby lost his boss, but the two had also been intimate. He'd lost Morgan, yet he was expected to be at work, bright and shiny to wait on Morgan's murderer the very next day. "Sit down, Rigs."

Rigby obeyed, moving to the golden table and chairs near the window. Morgan had eaten many a meal there, and I wondered if he had been permitted to eat there with her, as well. Judging by the hesitation in his step, I guessed this was his first time being invited to the table.

"My name is Rigby, your grace," he reminded me with a firm politeness, his posture rigid as he sat.

"Did you like it when I called you that before it all went south?"

He nodded, unable to make eye contact. "I looked forward to it every morning. Some days it was my only reminder that I was a person. But I don't deserve it now, so do not give me what I crave."

My bare feet brushed to the stone floor, placing me right in front of him so he couldn't look away. I bent over and leaned on the gold table, so we were on the same level. "Let's get a few things out in the open, okay? I was terrified when I first moved in here, but you and Demi made it all bearable. I get the whole master/slave mentality, and I understand you were just doing as you were ordered. However, I don't like that you let it all happen. You didn't love me. You also saw me mostly naked, and that's not cool." I sighed, closing my eyes. "But I killed your great love yesterday, so I'm thinking that makes us sort of even. I don't have the energy to be mad at you. It is what it is, and the whole thing was crappy."

"I did not love Morgan," he corrected me with an incredulous look. "I was addicted to her in the beginning, but that was never love. I was commanded to serve her, so I did. I saw many before me lose their heads because they did not perform for her whims with unswerving devotion. I did what I had to so I could survive, and help the other servants keep their heads." His guilty gaze flicked to me. "And if coming here every day and looking you in the eye to face all I've done to you is what's required of me, I'll do that, as well."

"Hey," I cooed, keeping my voice soft as my head tilted to the side. "I'm doing this all wrong. You're grieving, and me being here is making things all confusing for you. You should take some time to mourn. Deal with it all. Did you want a few days for a vacation? Go see your family or something?"

Rigs blinked at me in confusion. "I don't have family. The servants here are my family. I'll not leave them when things are still shifting. If I serve you, the rest of the household falls in line far easier."

"And I appreciate that, but you're going through a lot right now. Talk to me."

Rigby studied my features, seeking out any ulterior motive for a person to be kind. It broke my heart a little to see such a small gesture be so perplexing. "I'll not trouble you with a servant's musings. You're tired. You should go to sleep."

"I will, but you can unload while I wind down. I'm listening."

It took a few starts and stops, but eventually Rigby found his own voice. When the words came out of him, they were two steps forward, one step back. An admission of a feeling, and then backpedaling with oaths of loyalty to Avalon. I felt terrible for him, not being permitted to voice a simple feeling all these years. Now that he had the chance, he was all turned around.

After about ten minutes of easing himself in, Rigby began to unload years of abuse. He stared out the window, as if confessing to the quietness of nature all the depraved things Morgan had made him do. I'm not sure how either of us found the strength to make it through the conversation, but with my hand atop his, Rigby powered through, checking my eyes for judgment all the while as we sat at the gold table like old friends.

Therapy time came to an end when my tenth yawn couldn't be stifled. "Forgive me, your grace. I've taken advantage. Let me help you into your nightgown and fetch you some tea."

I waved off his thoughtfulness. "That's alright. I can get dressed myself. Man, you're about to have a lot of free time on your hands."

"It's my joy to serve you in whatever capacity you need. Shall I fetch you a new *soumettre*? Perhaps someone younger to suit your fancy?"

I gagged dramatically. "No, thanks. In fact, the existing

soumettres in the castle are officially freed. They can work in the castle for pay, or they can go back to their families. Whatever they like."

Rigby blinked like I'd said something crazy. "Freed?"

"Why not?"

"I don't know what to do with that," he admitted. "I'd like to stay on and serve the throne, if you'll have me."

"Of course, but it's your choice."

Rigby nodded, as if confused by the notion of choice. "Thank you, your grace. I'm certain a few of the servants would jump at the chance to warm your bed – freed or not."

"Sheesh. I don't need it floating around that I've picked up Morgan's bad habits. I'm engaged to Bastien." I winced. "If he'll still have me, that is. Ugh. Screw my life."

Rigby studied my labored movements. "Engaged to the Untouchable, yet Master Kerdik bathes you?"

I blushed, my neck shrinking. "He didn't bathe me. He just kept me company on the other side of the divide. Kerdik is my..." I struggled to find the right word. "Okay, fine. Kerdik's my one terrible crime. But that doesn't mean I'm sleeping around. I'm always either with my fiancé or my boyfr..." I cringed. "Please don't make me talk about this."

An amused smile played on the corners of Rigby's thin lips. "I'll be back with your tea."

27

LETTING HIM HOLD ME

My clothes had been brought down for me, so I sifted through them until I found the long, comfy dressing gown that was thin and not cumbersome. After all the blood, a simple white gown felt necessary – healing, in a way. Would that my insides were just as unblemished.

Rigby returned with a tea tray and a leather journal. "I brought this for you. I thought you might like to read some of Demi's poetry. I didn't think his family should read it. Some of his confessions about his time here were quite graphic. But if you would like to remember his love for you, this might help." When Rigby sensed my hesitance, he pressed on. "Everything we have belongs to the queen, so though Demi wrote in this, it was never his, and now belongs to you."

Something precious that Avalon hadn't managed to

stamp out whispered a softness through my heart. "Demi wrote poems about me." I spoke the words like they were evidence of the shattered parts of me that might always feel jagged and broken.

"Several. I thought they should remain with you, private as they are."

"Wow. I don't know what to say." Relief loosened my stiff shoulders that I didn't have to show my dyslexic cards too soon. "Thank you." I didn't want Bastien or Kerdik reading some other dude's love poems about me, and didn't want to sit through Lane or Judah's teasing that a boy had liked me, either. This is the problem with being dyslexic. You don't get to process something huge like that in private.

Rigby picked up a comb and motioned for me to sit in the golden chair at the table while I sipped my rose-scented tea. The hot liquid smelled comforting, but tasted like the nothing my lunch and dinner had been. He was careful with my curls, taking time on each tangle with no hint of the frustration I usually attacked my hair with. "If I may, your grace. See that you wear your dressing gown only in your bedroom. If the servants see you in this, I fear you may have more attention than you know what to do with."

I sniggered at his gentle teasing. "Alright. Thanks. There aren't all that many sleepwear options in Avalon."

When I finished my tea, I laid my head on the table, letting Rigby brush a scented oil through my waves while I tried to keep my eyes open. When he lifted me from the chair and carried me to the bed, my mouth opened in protest, but that was the most of it. I decided to put my pride aside and let Ribgy take care of me. After all we'd been through, I let myself off the hook for needing a pair of reassuring arms to situate my head on the down pillow.

My mother was dead, and I was starting to feel the low swings of that as my adrenaline and denial began to ebb. The horrible truths threw themselves at me, slamming me in the face as I closed my eyes. I hoped sleep would take me, for no reason other than to mute the onslaught of emotion I could feel beating at my internal walls.

I rolled onto one side, and then the other as Rigby busied himself about the room, turning out the larger lanterns and leaving only one taper by my bedside to light the bags under my eyes.

"Are you alright, your grace? Is the bed not to your liking? I can have the mattress changed out, if you wish. I'm afraid I've never slept before, so I cannot attest to its comfort as far as that aspect is concerned."

I shifted again, trying to shut my brain off, as my exhausted body was screaming at it to do. "The bed is gorgeous. It's like, bigger than a King-sized. I'm fairly certain I could fit all my problems in here stacked end to end, and still have room left over for a unicorn."

Rigby pulled a chair over and sat down in it, looking very much like a shrink as he studied the changes in my smile – or the disappearance of it altogether. "Tell me of the problems. It's my job to make sure the crown is easier to bear."

I debated going back and forth on the tamer subject matters, but it was late, so I went for the ugliest truth I knew. "I murdered my own mother. I'm afraid I'm turning into her. She saw something she wanted, and she buried her own family to get it. I'm the exact same."

Rigby didn't contradict me, which made me feel like he was actually listening. He took the time to process my fears instead of turning into a yes man I couldn't trust to be anything more than a royalty sycophant.

When he didn't respond, I pressed further into the wound as my stomach screamed at me for more of Bastien. "I'm a Vampire now, plus I've got all these other changes to me that at best, are a mixed bag. My eyeball changed color a little while ago. I don't know why that makes me saddest. I barely recognize myself anymore. Through all the ups and downs I always had me, right? Now there's barely enough pieces of me left to point to the original gangsta version."

"I would imagine those are normal things to be feeling right now. Let me ask, do you regret putting an end to Morgan, knowing all you do about her?"

My stomach growled, making me anxious as I tried desperately to not let the hunger pains taunt me. "I regret that my love did nothing. This small, childish part of me thought that if she just got to know me, all the bad things would stop being true. That we'd meet and we'd be instant girlfriends. She'd stop being a horrible person, and I'd have a mom I didn't have to steal, all because of my love." I clutched at my pillow as my stomach screamed once more. "My love was supposed to be special, but in the end it couldn't even save my own flesh and blood."

Rigby brought me a roll from my tray. "Here, little dove. Eat something. Maybe that'll help with the blood cravings. I confess, I don't know much about Vampires. They weren't around these parts back when the higher magic roamed free. Master Kerdik explained the basics of your condition, but I'm afraid I'm not much help." He rolled up his sleeve. "Would you like some of my blood?"

I blinked up at him in surprise. "Are you serious? You're really offering to let me cut you open and drink your blood?"

"I'm offering to help you with whatever you need. If it's blood, then take what you like."

I sat up and motioned him forward. He didn't renege, not even when I wrapped my arms around him and brought my mouth to the vulnerable spot where I'd feasted on Bastien.

Bastien! Just thinking his name made me hungrier.

Instead of biting, I placed a light kiss to Rigby's neck. "Thank you, but it has to be Bastien."

Rigby pulled back to press his lips to my forehead, sealing our re-friendship on a note of trust. He laid me down on the bed, taking my hand and massaging it with oil he found on the nightstand. He sniffed the bottle and grimaced. "I'll see to getting you new perfume. I don't want you smelling like Morgan. It doesn't suit you."

"Hey, Rigs?"

"Yes, my dove?"

"Tell me it all gets better. I don't care if it's a lie at this point." I let out a whine of pain as my stomach turned, calling for something I couldn't give it.

He swept the hair from my forehead tenderly. "It will get much, much better. I promise you."

"Thanks." My stomach growled, and the pain hit me enough to make me coil into the fetal position. "Have a good night, Rigs. You can go now. It's just going to be more of this. You don't need to stay for it."

Rigby glanced at the door, and then rose to lock it instead of leaving. He surprised me when he kicked off his shoes and climbed into the bed, scooting in behind me to spoon my curled body. I was torn between pushing him away and clinging to the life raft, scared as I was. His arm wrapped around me, linking his fingers through mine so I could squeeze him through the painful parts. "Until it all gets better, I'm here," he vowed.

I closed my eyes, willing myself not to burst into tears. That night, I let Rigby hold me together while my insides threatened to fall apart.

THE DEATH OF SUPERMAN

I awoke to a sharp sting on my hand. When my eyes opened, I realized that I was the culprit. I'd been gnawing on my knuckle like it was a chew toy while I slept, and had finally broken through the skin. Rigs wasn't in the room anymore, having left sometime in the night, no doubt to attend to more urgent matters than babysitting a grown woman.

Since I was alone and no one could see my crime, I lapped at my blood, noting the taste that wasn't as good as Bastien's, but certainly wasn't as acrid as Kerdik's. I sucked harder, my eyes rolling back. If this was to be my peanut butter and jelly when I'd been craving a real feast, I would take it. My free hand gripped my pillow while I drank my own blood, cutting a little deeper so I had more to fill my aching stomach.

When I wasn't quite so ravenous anymore, I got

dressed for the day, regretting very much that I didn't have a spare set of clothes I could actually be useful in. The pink gown that had been laid out for me showed off my shape. It didn't even have sleeves, but instead had these gold bands that went around my upper arms, with material that flowed down to my thighs. I was only pretty sure I was putting it all on correctly.

When Rigby came with my breakfast, I had already packed up four more boxes with treasure for my dad. I even found a tiny closet with his old things in it. I didn't go through them, but instead put them in the pile in the corner of Morgan's bedroom – all things to be taken home and given to my dad.

Rigby's eyebrows tented in the center when he saw me up and about. "Your majesty? I thought you were still asleep."

"I'm ready to get on with whatever it is I'm supposed to be doing today." I rubbed the back of my neck. "Sorry I sort of lost it last night. This whole Vampire thing is a little rough."

"There's nothing to be sorry for." He set the breakfast tray on the table and handed me a bowl of berries. "Here you are. I've never heard anyone's stomach growl quite as loud and as often as yours did last night. Are you quite sure you're alright? You look less ravenous."

"I am. Or I'm dealing with it, anyways. Thanks." I ate half the bowl of berries, wincing at the flavorless food. Though they looked amazing, they tasted like... nothing.

Utter and complete nothing. I ate for the sake of caloric intake, returning to my task once I'd finished. "Is Kerdik back?"

"He is. The grave's been filled, so that's a relief. He's... a bit moody, if I may be so impertinent as to comment on it."

"Kerdik? Moody? I don't believe it," I commented with a churlish grin. "I'll see what I can do, once I'm finished in here."

I requested the head of castle security be brought in, since Kerdik had vetted the staff for me. I gave him a list of things to see to: gather up the remaining healers and make sure they had all the provisions they needed to treat the wounded, get someone he trusted to start with a census to see how many people were actually still in the province, and organize the army to start with the homes closest to the castle and see that each family had all the help they needed. A message was also sent to Fabian to start making bread, which would be handed out to anyone who needed it while they dealt with the upset their land had suffered.

Rigby devoted the next three hours to helping me with my mother's things, boxing up gowns and keeping me company while I sussed through the remnants of Morgan's life.

"What do you think you're doing?" Kerdik's sharp voice came to me like the crack of a whip from the entrance to the bedroom. Rigby jumped to his feet and moved to the window, standing at attention.

I looked up at Kerdik from my position on the floor, my

dress fanned out around me as I thumbed through a box that held bracelets with jewels of every color in them. The corner of my mouth tugged upward at Kerdik's lack of a greeting. "Hello, Sunshine. Don't you look sweet today. I think it's that smile. Best part of waking up," I teased.

Kerdik rolled his eyes at me and stomped over to where I sat, hefting me up so he could assess whether or not the floor had... I dunno, broken all my bones or something. He was always so dramatic when I tried to do normal things. His eyebrows were furrowed together in concern. "You are the acting ruler of this province now. Do not test my patience by sitting on the floor like a peasant."

"You're such a love bug. It's nice to see you, too. How's Dad? Are the others home, yet?"

"They are, but only because I ported them there myself. They were making horrible time. Mortals can be ever so tedious."

"What's up in Province 10? Was Dad happy to get all the gifts I sent?"

Kerdik's expression was cautious. "He was more than grateful. He sent me for a few extra things he wasn't sure you knew to look for." Kerdik's eyes held a guarded note to them. "He said you might like to spend some more time here. After this, you should feel free to go to your home in Common."

My nose crinkled. "Well, I mean, the plan all along was for me to go back to my regular life. But I'll go home and say goodbye to him first, of course. What's going to happen to Province 1?"

"That's for you to decide, Queen Rosalie."

I blew out a loud raspberry at the ridiculous address. "Well, that's terrifying." Though, as the decision was offered to me, I mulled over the logistics. "Province 5 is closer to this place than Province 10. Plus we've got more people in Province 10 than we know what to do with. What do you think of Duke Lot?"

I could hear the pride in Kerdik's voice that I was taking this seriously. "I think it matters what *you* think of Duke Lot. Do you think him worthy of ruling over this many people in the throes of such upset?"

"I think if he's lasted this long standing against Morgan, he's got a handle on things I couldn't begin to understand."

"I think you're right. Shall I send word to Duke Lot?"

"Really? Yeah, that'd be great."

I expected Kerdik to ask one of my guards to send a carrier pigeon or something, but apparently he wanted things expedited. "I'll port there myself. Be back in a few minutes."

"Oh, seriously? Wow. Thanks, K." I barely got out the few words before he was gone. He got back just as I was finishing up boxing yet another load of my mother's things, and wondering how she'd feel about me touching them.

Kerdik frowned at me and lifted me from the floor

again. "Honestly, it's like you want to provoke me. Queens do not sit on the floor."

"Is that so? Well the jig is up, then. I must not be a real queen."

Kerdik's eyes darted to the ceiling and back to steady himself against my flippant response to his scolding. "It's done. Duke Lot is getting ready to come here to talk about the future for Province I. He should be here this evening."

"Oh, wow. That was quick. Thank you." Relief flooded over me at the thought that most of the loose ends were being tied up and wrapped in a nice, non-cumbersome bow.

"How are you feeling?" He didn't ask permission, but squeezed my cheeks so my jaw dropped open, peering into my mouth, as if inspecting an animal.

I batted his hand away with a frown. "I'm alright. Found out that if I drink a little of my own blood, I'm not quite so miserable with hunger."

His eyebrow raised. "Interesting. I didn't know that."

"I think I'm going to take a break from packing and go help outside with whatever you're doing, K. That alright with you, Rigs?"

Rigby bowed. "Whatever pleases you, your majesty."

I couldn't help the labored sigh that escaped my lips at Rigby's complete obeisance. "Cool."

"No," Kerdik ruled. "You'll stay in the castle until it's time for you to go back to Common."

I quirked my eyebrow at him, demanding an explanation. "You want to add a 'this is why I'm acting like a controlling lunatic' to the conversation? I have to head back to Province 10 after I'm done here anyways. Hello, Judah's there."

"I'll bring Judah to you, and whatever else you need. You're not to return to Province 10 ever again."

I balked at the command that made absolutely no sense to me. "Come again? I'm not going to duck out without saying goodbye to everyone. I have friends and family there, Kerdik, plus a little throne that I want to make sure doesn't need me before I split."

Kerdik's face was composed, but I could see a storm brewing behind his eyes. "Lane would lie to you in this situation, but I don't have a lie you'd believe."

I pinched the bridge of my nose. "Rigs, could you give us a second?" When Rigby bowed and excused himself from the room, I stared up at Kerdik, arms akimbo. "Alright, then. Out with it."

Kerdik's gaze combed my features with a palpable pain, now that we were alone. "Must you always look so stunning when you're about to hate me?"

"Why would I hate you?" I asked, inching away warily.

"I would hate the person who brought the news that broke my heart."

"Is everyone okay? What happened? Where's Lane? Bastien? Is he alright?" Panic flooded through me. "My dad? Judah? Who?!"

"Sit down, darling."

"No." I was firm that if my world was about to change yet again, that I face it on my feet.

"Oh, joy. You're starting off stubborn. I can tell this is going to go smashingly."

I wanted to shake the truth out of Kerdik. "Tell me everything right now."

Kerdik drew in a deep breath as he fished for the right place to start. Every second that ticked by was one he was seriously gambling on my self-control. I was about to thrash him when finally he began to explain. "Years ago, before the higher magic was bottled up, Faîte had a whole slew of different problems. That's why Brìghde, Cailleach and I took most of the magic away. We stripped our nations down to the barest essentials so they could see what was important, and not let too many problems cloud what could be great about who they were, and could be."

"I know all this. Fast forward to the part that's got my stomach twisting in knots." My tummy growled for Bastien's blood, right on schedule.

Kerdik glanced toward the door, as if he'd very much like to make good use of it. "Back then, the darker creatures were known for their basest needs, and not much more. If you were a Dullahan, that's all you were known as. Those were your contributions to Faîte." He massaged his temples. "The Dullahan were from Éireland, so mostly harrowing tales of woe traveled here. Avalon got a very stilted view of the dark magic."

"Dude, I can't remember what a Dullahan is. It's like,

the thirtieth weird thing we've talked about in the last twenty-four hours."

"A headless horseman. Rides around looking for heads to collect. Once they stop riding on their steed, someone in Avalon dies." He shook his head at the rabbit trail. "It makes no difference. Those didn't exist in Avalon, but the fearful tales reached our shores all the same. There are laws – old laws – about such creatures. One is that they're not allowed on royal ground, which means they can't be on the palace property."

"Okay. I'll keep an eye out for any headless horsemen trying to ride around in the backyard."

"This is your province by birthright, technically, so you can run it how you choose. Kick out whoever displeases you. And it wasn't just the Dullahan; it was all of the darker creatures that couldn't be tamed." He shot me furtive looks and kept glancing away uncomfortably. "The higher magic has reached Province 10, and people are starting to be affected."

"Oh, yikes. The fog made it all the way over there? That's not good. I bet they're all pretty scared. If this signing over the land to Lot thing can be wrapped up tonight, I'll go back home tomorrow and see if I can help Dad out."

"Your father's decided the old laws should be upheld, so he's exiled any of the Dullahan or any other creatures that have started to form since the magic was set loose."

I shrugged. "Okay. Am I supposed to be kicking people

out or something? That feels off. I mean, I just got here. And besides, are the horsemen actually going around taking people's heads off, or are they just collecting the already severed ones? Because I've got to tell you, I don't have a problem if people want to clean up heads off the ground so I don't have to."

Kerdik threw his hands in the air. "Do you really not understand what I'm trying to tell you?"

I shrugged. "What?"

"You cannot return to your father because you're a Vampire now!"

"Huh?" My nose crinkled. "Well, explain the situation to him. I'm not a legit bloodsucker, latching onto any random Joe I can find. It's only Bastien who's affected. If Bastien was the one to kick me out, I would understand. But my dad's not in danger from me. Did you tell him that?"

"Urien well understands the difference between the two kinds of Vampires." Kerdik swallowed the lump in his throat, his eyes on his shoes. "His rule still stands. Those affected by the darkness are to be exiled. He's allowed for them to vacate their homes peacefully, but the announcement is going out tomorrow that they must leave and never come back to Province 10."

"But that's my home! I mean, I live there!"

Kerdik shook his head. "No, darling. You don't."

My nostrils flared in defiance. "You're lying to me. My

dad loves me! Did you tell him his daughter is affected by this stupid edict?"

"I did. I pleaded with him, threatened him and did everything to try and make him see, but he's as stubborn as his daughter. He's doing what he thinks he needs to in order to keep his kingdom protected. You know he rules in black and white, with no room for gray."

"That's bullshit!" I raged. "I'm not a threat to his kingdom! Lane and I are the ones who gave him Province 10! Where does Lane stand in all of this?"

"She doesn't have a say in it, because she's firm that she's leaving Avalon with you. It's Urien's call. It's his province to look after, however he chooses."

My cheeks were hot, yet I felt pale and exposed. My stomach was screaming at me for Bastien, making my thoughts harder to put in order. "I just sent him buckets of jewels and whatnot, and he kicks me out? I don't get it!"

Kerdik folded his arms over his chest. "I brought every single piece back, down to the last coin. I told your little friend Judah to start packing his things, too. When I go back, it will only be to gather up what belonged to you and leave. Judah is... He's quite distraught about Urien's rule. He demanded I take him to you at once, but I left him with Urien in the fruitless hope that perhaps he could reason with the king on your behalf. Your little companion is annoying and doesn't know when to shut up, which makes him the perfect person to leave in the castle with Urien."

My fists clenched at my sides. Had I the psychic nature

power that Kerdik did, the walls would've trembled with my rage. "Take me home."

Kerdik's chin lowered as he shook his head. "Perhaps I should've lied to you instead, told you he'd died or something. That's what Lane would've done to spare your feelings."

When the next words flung out of me, they were shouted with a volume I couldn't control. "I will not go another twenty years without my dad! I won't let him not want me in his house! I wanted a real parent for too long to take this lying down. I didn't ask for this! I was attacked by the higher magic! I'm not hurting his kingdom. I don't understand!"

When Kerdik's arms banded around me, I struggled against him in anger, furious that this was the hand I'd been dealt. "He's doing what he thinks is best. If he makes exceptions for you, then all the fathers who are losing their children will revolt, demanding to keep their families together."

"You mean like good dads are supposed to do? How dare they want to love their own children. Let me go!"

"Not until you calm down. Darling, I tried to reason with him, but he won't budge."

"So, what? I just lose my family and my home? I lose the friends I made there? I helped rebuild that province! So did the other people he'll be kicking out. Province 10 was supposed to be a haven for the outcasts, and now they're pushing the lepers out?

Where are they supposed to go? What are they supposed to do?"

Kerdik didn't answer; he simply held me while my heart bled in time with my tear ducts. I couldn't see a thing – so thick were my tears that streamed down my face. Blindness spooked me, so I thrashed without direction. My chin jerked around as I screamed in fear and heart-wrenching agony. I was furious that after all I'd gone through – avenging my dad's stolen years by murdering the woman who'd enslaved him – it amounted to nothing. I wasn't special enough to warrant grace in a sticky situation. I wasn't loved enough to be welcomed into my father's house – the house I'd brought him into. I was leaveable, which tore a hole through my chest that was too big a void for anything to fill. It felt physical, this hole, like everyone could see the gaping wound I would carry for the rest of my days.

My vision didn't clear, but after my meltdown, my head started to. My fists clenched at Kerdik's back, and I pounded into him with every sentence that tumbled out of my gritted teeth. "I did everything I could to give him back his life, and this is the thanks I get? I'm not good enough to live in my father's house?"

"No, darling. That's not it. Urien's wrong, but he still loves you."

"Love doesn't feel like this!" I yelled, furious that anyone might misconstrue kicking their own daughter out as love. "I stayed with him while he was in his coma. I did everything he asked of me when he came to! I built up our kingdom – not his, *ours*!"

"I know. He's shortsighted. He's seeing the shifting world in black and white, so the gray doesn't take over."

"If he'd been infected with the Vampire juice, no way would I have turned away from him! Love doesn't look away; it runs toward the pain! He knows I'm broken, and this is what he does?" I let out a few cuss words so angry and foul, Kerdik flinched at my venom. The child that was rapidly dying inside my soul howled, "Superman would never do this to me!"

Kerdik sounded panicked at my agony. His best guy friend and his girlfr—or whatever I was, were parting ways. "Darling, give him time. He'll see the error in it all when he realizes he has to live without your smile."

"He's *choosing* to live without my smile; it's not something he has to do!" My voice turned mournful and my breathing came in shallow pants as I pounded my heartache into Kerdik's shoulders with my balled fists. "My smile isn't magical. It doesn't heal things or make my dad love me. My dad doesn't love me! My mom didn't love me! Why don't my parents want me? What did I do wrong?"

"Obviously nothing, Rosie. Breathe, darling. You have to calm down. You're going to make yourself faint."

A new level of terror shot through me. "Is that why Lane left to go back home? Is she done with me, too?" Before Kerdik could answer, a horrible wail rose up in me at the thought that my Lane might write me off, as well. I'd put her through too much – the dyslexia, the fighting in school, the bills – all of it had been bearable, but now that I was a monster I'd finally pushed her over the edge. I was too much for my mom, and now I would lose her, too.

Kerdik bloomed a flower out from the center of his palm, and then crushed it in his fist to release the lilac and somehow buttery fragrance. "Inhale, darling. Take a breath. You're losing it. Lane won't turn her back on you; she already knows you're a Vampire. She only left you here because I made her. She needs to say goodbye to Province 10. As soon as she does that, she'll be here to collect you, and take you away from all of this."

Through my gusty, gaspy breaths, I slowly began to calm, hiccupping through my pain as my knees began to weaken and my body went slack.

Kerdik swore. "I'm sorry, my love. That's on me. That was too strong for you to inhale all at once. Forgive me. I'll fix it." He scooped me up in his arms before I hit the floor. I couldn't see a thing through my tears, but I knew Kerdik had me. He sat on the bed and kissed my forehead, washing my face, which revived me enough to regain control of my neck.

I blinked up at him with wet lashes, utterly distraught and completely destroyed. "My dad doesn't love me," I whispered.

Kerdik captured my vision with a tender expression. "Then he's a fool. I knew the very first moment I saw you running at me in that storm that you were worth moving the stars in the sky to keep you close to me. Urien is scared, and people make all sorts of foolish choices when they're afraid." Kerdik kissed my damp cheek. "Trust me when I tell you that this will be the regret he never outlives."

"But *I* have to live with it," I croaked. "He's afraid of me, so I get gutted." Too many more things bubbled up inside of me, willing to spill out so at least one other person would have to share in my agony. Instead, I closed my mouth, locking the pain tight inside my chest.

"What can I do? How can I make it better?"

I shook my head, unsure how to open my mouth without a whole bag of crap spilling out. I settled on leaning into his warmth, and rested my head against his shoulder until the pain dulled to a deafening ache. We sat like that for several long minutes, letting the silence say things neither of us were willing to voice. Finally I took his hand and pressed it over my heart. "Tell me it'll stop hurting someday."

Kerdik's eyes were hollow, but he didn't miss a beat with, "It will stop hurting someday." His skin started to fog over with a brush of crimson, letting me know that it never would. Kerdik lied to try and heal me, and I loved him a little bit more for the sin.

29

BLOODY MAD FOR BASTIEN

My hands were shaking with hunger for Bastien as I tried to change into a clean dress. By the time Lot arrived, and I'd ruined three dresses by crying all over them. My eyes teared up again, and I tried to breathe through the panic that came at being suddenly blinded by blood. I felt the red dribble down my cheeks, and I knew I didn't have any more clean water in the basin to wash my face with. Instead of flailing and trying to feel my way around for a place to sit, I dropped down onto all fours like a dog, so my tears wouldn't ruin the fourth dress I'd put on that day. I breathed through my teeth, shutting my eyes so the blindness would be my choice, instead of my affliction. To make matters worse, I was so hungry that I licked at my own tears, which didn't taste great, and didn't totally satiate my hunger, but helped me to be able to focus on the task at hand.

When a knock sounded at the door, I tried to keep my voice light. "Just a minute."

"Darling? You're to receive your guest now. Rigby's giving him a tour of the grounds to buy you some time."

"Cool. I'll be out in a second." I fumbled around until I found the hem of one of my ruined dresses. Dabbing at my face and eyes didn't let me see perfectly, but it was good enough to get me to the basin, so I could splash on some bloody water. When I could finally see without the red filter, I peered down at the bowl, my heart racing with shame and dread of being randomly struck blind by my own tears. My stomach screamed for Bastien in every way. Self-loathing trickled over me as I lifted the salad bowl-sized porcelain vessel and tipped it to my lips. I hated everything I'd become as the crimson water flooded my mouth.

I set the bowl back down before my quaking hands dropped the whole thing and I ruined yet another dress. I moved to the door and rolled my shoulders back, raising my chin so I appeared to be the kind of girl who didn't sob on all fours in her bedroom when she had real responsibilities to attend to. I opened the door to greet Kerdik with what I hoped was a convincing smile. "Hey, sorry about that. I'm ready now."

Kerdik turned me around and marched me back into the bedroom, sucking the remnants of the filthy water into his palms and filling it with clean water. "You've obviously been crying. You look like you broke your nose and took a beating to your mouth. There's blood smeared everywhere."

My shoulders slumped that my show of confidence could be seen right through. "I'm sorry. I thought I was hiding it well enough."

Kerdik eyed my dresses that looked as if they should be worn by horror movie extras, and lifted one off the pile on the floor. He wetted a clean edge and tenderly scrubbed my face, eyeing my tight expression. "You're hungry," he observed. "Bastien will be back soon enough. Tomorrow evening, in fact."

I stiffened as my stomach screamed like a toddler. "I thought he would be back tomorrow morning."

"He's proved quite useful in rounding up some of the Vampires. The rabid ones are biting the populace, so it's important we act quickly with all of this."

I gave him a stiff nod, but kept my bleat of distress to myself. "Do you have that vial of his blood still?"

Kerdik's jaw was tight. "I do. Are you certain you need it?"

I wanted to power through, but I was too emotional to add starvation on top of the misery. "I do. Please."

Kerdik nodded, his face solemn. "Very well." He pulled out the vial of blood from his pocket and uncorked it, releasing the pure scent of Bastien into the air. I groaned at the smell of his blood as it called to me. "Easy, now. This is all there is. Once you finish it, there won't be any more. Can you accept that?"

I nodded, desperate to get my hands on the blood. "Please, Kerdik."

He was careful with the small container of blood, tipping it to my lips. "Slowly."

My hands shook with need, sweat beading on my forehead as I tried to restrain myself to drink like a human, and not like a greedy animal. When the red liquid flowed into my mouth, I let out a scared noise of relief that broke my heart. This was my greatest solace and joy – my fiancé's blood.

But oh, the sweet ecstasy it was. I groaned, licking the vial after I'd swallowed the shot. The blood hummed through my whole body, awakening nerves and sensations I wanted Bastien there for. My lashes fluttered shut, and my hand went to the back of Kerdik's head to grip his hair tight in my fist.

He pressed his forehead to mine, kissing my cheeks and sending little pitter patters of attraction through me. The kisses married with the blood, and for a second, I debated begging Kerdik to throw me on the bed and make love to me. I was flying high, smack in the middle of a full-on meltdown of depression. I bit down on my lower lip through the temptation, clenching my thighs together through the waves of need.

"Easy," he warned as I shuddered against him. My knees gave out as a ripple of lust washed through me, but Kerdik held me firm to his chest until I was able to breathe through it all and get myself under control.

"I can't think! This is…" I licked my lips and tongued the vial again – the mere smell of the blood turning my spine to jelly.

"I deserve a medal for this. You wouldn't protest if I tore your dress off you right now, and yet I'm expected to be the adult in this situation." He brushed his nose across mine, the simple touch driving me insane with need so much that my knees buckled. Kerdik held me up, pressing parts of my body to his that started to purr with need.

"Kerdik, my body's freaking out!"

Kerdik smirked at me with unabashed affection. "This is all part of the bond you'll share with Bastien. You'll feed from him, and then you'll be able to make love to him." His tone turned darker as he slipped the sleeve off my shoulder. He spoke into my skin, the sweep of his lips making me cry out with desire. "But when it's my blood you're drinking after his life is over and done, we won't stop making love for weeks on end. Every touch will be exactly this. You'll never tire of my affections."

We managed to extract ourselves from each other, both of us panting as he gave me the time for my mind to adjust and my body to calm down. It took a solid ten minutes for me to straighten up, and talk myself through the freak show that my body was now. I mean, it was just a little taste, and I'd been practically vibrating with need.

I rolled back my shoulders and straightened my hair, embarrassment coloring my cheeks. "Sorry about that."

"Absolutely never a need to apologize for giving me a glimpse at what's in store for us. I love you, Rosie."

My mouth curved into a small smile. "I love you, too. Thanks for being cool about all that. I'm still adjusting, I guess." I glanced down at my gown. "Am I princess enough yet?" I feared I might look more like the panting mistress I was.

"Always their princess," he said, kissing my cheek. Then he pecked my lips and whispered, "Always my queen. Where's your crown, love?"

I shrugged. "I don't wear one."

"The one I made you. I know it was left here, but can you find it?"

I rubbed my stomach, which had dulled from a growling roar to a kitten mewling for more. My gut was harder to hear over the constant pangs of hunger, but eventually I heard it. I spun around and marched into Morgan's closet, taking the secret false door route to the place she'd stashed it. The white gold was beautiful, as were the diamonds and aquamarine gems that shimmered out at me as if they held their own natural glow. Despite everything, I couldn't look away from the beauty. I picked it up, but couldn't bring myself to put it on my head. It felt wrong somehow, like I was telling everyone I could afford designer jeans or something.

Kerdik sensed my dilemma and slid the crown from my fingers, resting it on my head as he'd done the first time I'd worn the stunning piece. He twisted my hair around it, blooming baby's breath between the crown of braids Rigby had done for me.

"Tell me I'm enough without the crown," I breathed in a pained whisper.

"You're enough without the crown, but you'll wear this one because I made it for you, and I want to see my love wearing my gift. Always their princess; always my queen." He pressed a kiss to the vulnerable spot behind my ear. "Come, now."

30

NEEDING A LITTLE LOT

Kerdik offered me his elbow, moving us slowly out of the bedroom, past a bored Maurice and through the hallways to the visiting room Bastien and I had reunited in. I remembered well the sight of Mad sitting uncomfortably on the pristine cold and crimson furniture, offering me his hand in marriage as a way out of my crappy situation.

Lot had also offered to marry me at the Holy Crap, Rosie's Alive! party. I hoped he wasn't pissed at me for turning down his friendly offer.

Lot rose from his seat, flanked by two guards wearing the blue and black of his province. He cast me a sweet smile before he bowed his head to me. "Your majesty, it's a privilege to see you again. Thank you for the invitation."

"It's good to see you, Lot." Before I could stop myself, I

offered up an awkward, "Sorry I look like this. I know it's weird."

Duke Lot smiled with a gentle dance in his eyes for me. "Not at all. Even when we traveled together to search for the Jewels of Good Fortune, I knew you were destined to wear a crown."

Rigby covered over his smirk with his hand and cleared his throat, motioning to the chair he stood next to. "Your majesty."

I tried to remember to sit up straight and play the part of someone who had their crap together.

Lot was dressed in his formal gear, complete with a small crown and a sash. He looked like a royal Ken doll. "I hope I'm not the first to congratulate you on your victory in winning this land for yourself."

I blinked at him with a note of melancholy that seeped through. "You are, as a matter of fact. Thank you."

Kerdik lowered me gently to the chair, tucking a lock of hair behind my ear in an almost territorial way Lot did not miss as he took his seat. Kerdik sat in a gold chair next to me, leaning back as he carefully observed the mild exchange.

My posture was rigid when I asked Lot's guards and Rigby to please shut the doors for me and give us a minute so the three of us could be alone. When Lot's guards protested, he waved them off. "It's alright. The queen is an old friend of mine, and if Master Kerdik wishes me dead, there's precious little the two of you could do to stop him."

"How very true," Kerdik nodded.

When we were alone, Lot asked for details of Morgan's death, and the whole nine yards. When I got to the part about the higher magic, Lot's head bowed with sadness. "Your messenger informed me as much, but I've not seen any of the dark creatures manifest in my land. Will my province be affected? I haven't seen anything to indicate we might be in danger."

Kerdik shook his head. "No. Brìghde and I blew the magic eastward, which means your province was skipped over. But Province 10 was hit, Province 1, and I assume the magic is on its way to its home in Éireland right about now."

I decided not to beat around the bush. "I don't want to live in Faîte anymore, Lot. I don't belong here. I've got a life to return to." Not much of one, granted, but I had a chance at boredom there. Beautiful, blissful boredom. Here, it was a barrage of death threats and bloody knives. No thanks.

Lot was quiet for a few beats. "I cannot say I'm surprised, but may I say that I'm a little sad that Avalon doesn't get to keep its fair Rose?"

"Thank you. That's very sweet."

He touched his chin, looking like a dashing noble even in thought. "You're marrying Bastien, I hear. Will he be going with you?"

I tossed him a smirk. "That's the thing about married couples."

Lot inclined his head to me. "Congratulations, Rosie.

Truly. Bastien is a great man, and you deserve the very best."

"Thanks, dude." I took in his sincerity, and wished a friend like him for all men and women everywhere. Lot was unselfish, kind and saw past the hype to who you truly were. "You're a good guy."

Lot sat straighter in his chair. "Which leads us to talk of business. Province 1 will merge with Province 10, I assume?"

"No. That's actually why I wanted to talk to you. King Urien's putting out an edict kicking out everyone who's been affected by the dark magic." I kept my chin level to the ground, feigning that I had my crap together. "I don't agree with this. Sure, the violent ones need to be dealt with, but the others should be able to live as normal of lives as they can."

Lot's blond eyebrows pulled together in consternation. "Well, obviously I agree with that. King Urien's really casting out all the victims?"

I nodded. "I won't hand more land and power over to a kingdom who does that. I want to merge Province 1 with someone who will take care of the people who've been jerked around by Morgan, and now this new magic. It won't be easy, but they deserve to feel safe."

"And you're sure you can't stay to give them that?"

I shook my head sadly. "I can't even give myself that." I lifted the edge of my upper lip to show him my slightly longer incisor. "I caught myself a case of the crap magic, so

I can't go live with my dad. I need to get out of here, Lot. Seriously. This was never my home. I've given enough to Avalon. I shanked my own mom to end all the craziness, and now my dad's kicking me out of my home because I caught a nasty Vampire virus."

Lot gasped, a wave of fear cresting over his features when it started dawning on him that some of the dangers would never leave the land. "No!"

Kerdik held up his hand. "She's an *Attelage*, obviously, and she's already bonded with Bastien. She's of no harm to anyone but him."

Lot settled back in his chair, but his eyes were wide and concerned as he studied me in this new light. "I can see why you care so much for their plight now. How can I help?"

I softened, my shoulders relaxing that I'd chosen the right person for the job. "I want you to merge with Province 1, but only if you promise to welcome in the refugees my da—King Urien is kicking out. They need someone kind and good, and I've known you to be only those things."

Lot put his hand to his chest at my grand words. "Thank you, my queen. I feel the same way about you. Of course I can do that. I'm honored. Whole wars are fought to gain land from a neighboring country. That you're handing this to me with so few stipulations is a wonder I'm not worthy of."

Kerdik stood. "Then get worthy."

I tried to keep the exchange civil, ignoring Kerdik's tartness towards Lot. "The *Attelage* Vampires should be allowed to live their lives as normally as they can."

"Agreed. What of the *Farouche*? They're a danger, Rosie."

I nodded, my hands in my lap. "I'd like them to be put in the dungeon until a cure can be found. They can live off of animal blood donated from the butchers after they do their daily slaughters. I'd like a system worked out to where one gallon of animal blood equals a tax break." I didn't turn my head to look at Kerdik, but could see in my periphery that he was holding back a smile of appreciation at my ruling.

Lot blinked at me. "And if no cure can be found?"

"I'm sure they prefer imprisonment to death." I tilted my head to the side. "So soon you're giving up hope?"

"No. It'll be done as you wish it."

"Thank you. The people need to have a spirit of compassion for their fellow man. They need to take care of their neighbors, especially when their friends can't look after themselves anymore."

"I can appreciate the logic of that."

Kerdik leaned over and kissed my cheek. "You'll move your kingdom here, Duke. This is a larger and far more well-cared-for piece of land. I'll get started on setting up the aqueducts here." Kerdik brushed his fingers over my knuckles, sending a shudder of desire through me I tried to quell. His voice was serious with promise. "If this is to be your legacy, I'll see it grander than any of the others."

I caught Kerdik's hand and pressed it to my face, indulging in the feel of his skin on mine. "You don't have to do that."

"Say that after you see the fountain I'm going to build you." Kerdik met Lot's eyes in a warning. "That Rosie thinks you can do this speaks highly of you. I'll set up the land so your people have running water instead of a localized well system, as they do now. I'll make sure your land is fruitful enough to sustain the civilians and refugees. After that, however, do not rely on me to make this place great. I'll only be back every few years to check on Rosie's land. It's to you to defend my love's legacy. See that you don't disappoint me. I don't do well with disappointment."

Lot rose and bowed his head to Kerdik. "As you wish it, Master Kerdik. I'll keep her province afloat, and I'll even return it to her better than she left it, if she should ever come back to us." Lot reached out and clutched my hand, his smile brightening the whole room, as was his charm. "Thank you, my queen. Thank you for this. I'll honor your request, and all the good you've brought to Avalon."

I felt like a hug was the thing to do in a situation like this, but I was afraid that if I indulged in anything that softened me, I would burst into tears all over again. Apparently, only a hundred times a day is my hard limit.

My stomach grumbled an angry tune, frustrated that Bastien was so far from me. "Sorry. Did you want a tour of the castle? I mean, you can live wherever you like, but if you want to stay here, it's all yours."

"Here," Lot ruled without hesitation. "You've not been to Province 5. This is quite the step up. But it's yours, should you return to Avalon. Is that clear? I don't want you to think you and your future husband don't have a home in this world. Should you come back to us, Province 1 is yours to rule as you see fit, and this is the home you'll stay in."

This was the time for a hug, and I couldn't hold back. I braced myself against my impending tears and flung myself into Lot's arms. "That was the perfect thing to say. Thank you. If I ever come back, I call the top bunk."

Lot chuckled, squeezing me as tight as his well-bred manners would allow. "Anything you like, sweet girl. Come now, show me the home I'm to keep watch over for you." Lot extended his elbow to me, bowing to Kerdik, who excused himself to put his finishing touches on my kingdom so I could finally leave Avalon behind.

31

LEAVING AVALON ONCE AND FOR ALL

"*H*oney, you need to calm down." It was the tenth time Reyn had said as much to Lane, but she was in no mood to listen. They were both healing from significant wounds, so they cantered on the same horse, which meant their back and forth didn't catch much of a break.

"This is me calm. I swear, if I wasn't bent on leaving Avalon, I'd rage against Urien so hard, he wouldn't know what hit him." For the fifteenth time that day, Lane turned to me and said, "You know none of this is your fault, right, babe? Urien made a bad call. The second we cross over, he'll regret it."

"Uh-huh."

Draper chimed in with a vehement, "Good riddance to any father who turns his back on his own kid."

Bastien didn't say anything, but squeezed me around

the ribs, warming my cold insides. He could feel how down in the depths I was, yet despite it all he didn't turn his back on my pain. Not when I'd begged him to leave me after I drank from him at our reunion. Not even after I told him that I was an outcast in my own land now. Not even after he'd seen the fountain Kerdik had built in Province 1, marking the land as mine.

I was marked, alright. The fountain was enormous – easily three stories tall. There was the crew in all our glory with water pouring down us as we stood in various poses of fight and heroism. Lane, Draper and Reyn with their crowns, then Bastien, Kerdik and me, with Lot standing a little ways apart to the side.

The intricacy of the sculpture would make even Michelangelo green with envy. However, that wasn't the buzz around the province. *I* was the scandal. My likeness was carved in marble in the center of the fountain. Of all things, my nipples were displayed prominently through the thin drapery effect of my dress, and stood proudly to declare to the nation that yes, I am a woman.

Lane and Draper had been none too pleased about that one.

Bastien's stone likeness stood to the right and slightly in front of me, looking fierce in his burly protection of my family. Kerdik, that sneaky snake, carved himself with an arm wrapped around my waist from behind, claiming and clutching.

My face was... well, I can't remember ever making that

face. It was fierce and noble, my chin raised as if to say, "Screw you, opposition. Come and get it."

My nipples were sending the "come and get it" message as well, but apart from a shouting match with Kerdik, Bastien had decided he was going to let that one go.

Bastien stuck by me, holding me in the quiet moments when I couldn't find my voice to tell him I was screaming inside. That's the thing about the man you take with you through multiple worlds. Wherever I landed, I was grateful I had him.

I hadn't cried at all today, and part of me knew my vulnerable parts had iced over. It had been days, actually. When I'd kissed Rigby goodbye that morning, he'd teared up, but I remained tucked inside myself. I'd hit some sort of pain threshold I couldn't come back from.

"Do ye think I could convince a few stone smithies to carve out a sculpture of me?" Link squeezed his pectoral muscle. "My glorious breasts deserve to be commemorated just as much as Rosie's do."

Bastien cringed. "I'm about to turn around just so I can tear that stupid thing down."

"I'm with you, man," Judah nodded, his face stony. "More than I ever needed to see of you, Ro."

Link sniggered as we neared the compound that held the entrance to Common. Such a different experience it was riding in, than sneaking out with death at our heels. "Now, now. Whenever we miss our fair lass, all we'll have to do is look up and see her... *personality* beaming out at us."

Lane was in heavy mama bear mode, and shouted Link's ear off until he finally gave up on his lame jokes. Link was the only one who treated me as he always did. Crass though he was, there was a certain comfort to it. Everyone else spoke softly to me, and helped me with the simplest things as though I was too delicate for carrying my own pack. The strangest part about it all was that I let them. I didn't have my usual independence and fight. Though I'd struggled tooth and broken nail to break free of Avalon, now that we were on the brink of that goal being realized, I felt unsettled. I wanted to leave, but not like this. Not with a dad who didn't want me, a land that needed healing, and a boyfr... a Kerdik who would keep part of my heart with him in Avalon.

Kerdik's ring sparkled on my finger, with Bastien's on my left hand. I felt like a fraud sporting such luxuries while wearing jeans and a tank top. Bastien had me pick a gem from the treasury, and bought the gold to have it made into an engagement ring. It was a simple diamond, square-cut to match my aquamarine, though a slight bit larger. Bastien compared the stones side by side to make sure his was bigger. Insert your standard penis insecurity implications here.

Bastien dismounted and checked the area for signs of a threat. Though the army belonged to me and Lot now, I guess, we were all groomed to expect opposition. Mad's hands reached up to help me down after he'd swung Annabelle to the ground. He didn't say a word, and didn't need me to fill the silence, either. Mad seemed to get that there weren't words, so he didn't press me for them. He reached for Annabelle's tiny hand, who was already stretching out her arm to connect to her Papa. Try as he might to shake the little girl, they needed each other, and had a slightly more hopeful fate now that they were together.

Judah wasn't too keen on the compound. "Definitely a better experience when you're about to walk in with permission rather than being dragged out kicking and screaming. Still." He shuddered, moving closer to Lane and me.

Lane's arms moved easily around Judah, but mine stayed put. I don't know why I couldn't bring myself to hug my bestie. I suppose if I had actual comfort to give anyone, I'd keep a little for myself.

Link, Mad and Bastien drew their swords while Draper and Reyn readied their knives. Link led the way with his chest barreled and his voice booming. "Make way for Duchess Elaine and the Avalon Rose!"

The doors swung open, greeting us with the strangest sight. Lining the hallway of the compound were hundreds of soldiers, each standing at attention and saluting us. I stumbled back, but Mad caught me before I fled. "This is your due. Best not run from it."

I'd only met the new Captain of the Guard once two

days ago when Rigby had arranged a formal sit-down. His name was David, and he had a no-personality way about him that made for a tough leader who was to be respected. David, Lot and I had sat down and discussed how things were to be run in Avalon, and how the soldiers were to behave. We even included punishments that would be carried out if the soldiers were found to be lacking in the protect-and-serve capacity. Lot and I actually made a pretty decent team, and each night that I'd fallen asleep, I kept that small amount of peace tucked in my heart. I wasn't abandoning Avalon; I was giving them a ruler I trusted.

David bowed his head to me as we entered the compound. Reyn, Lane and Judah were visibly trembling at the trauma they'd endured under the army's banner they now walked right past. We moved through the hallways, not saying a word as we marched to the foot of the well we were to climb up.

I don't know why I hoped Kerdik would be there. We'd said our goodbyes last night. They were solemn, and filled with shortly spoken promises that clipped off whole anthems we wanted to express to each other. But the truth is, we knew it already. I knew what pedestal he put me on, and he knew what he meant to me. He promised to visit Avalon at least once a year to make sure everything was okay.

"Only once a year?" I'd said. "But this is your home."

Kerdik shook his head sadly. "There's nothing for me

here if you're not in Avalon. I need to leave for a while. Get some perspective, some space." He'd leaned in and quickly kissed my cheek. "Now tell me you'll have a grand life with Bastien, and that you'll come home to me when it's over."

I'd nodded, banding my arms around my middle. "I promise." I'd craned my neck to gaze up at him. "Thank you. Love like yours? I've never met anyone like you." I'd looked down at my shoes and bit down on my lower lip. "But if you find someone while I'm gone, I'll understand."

Kerdik cast aside our composed farewell and jerked me to him, staring down into my wide eyes with intensity that, even a day later, still made my heart flutter. "There will be no one else. Until you come home to me, my heart will remain in two places." Then he'd kissed me, long and passionate. Just messy enough to break us both into a million nonfunctional pieces. "I love you, Rosie. Never doubt that you are the beauty who gave me back my heart."

My hand wound through his blue hair, studying it and memorizing every follicle. "I love you, too."

One last kiss and he'd vanished, leaving me with a gaping wound I well deserved.

Bastien tore me a new one after that, but the fight quickly died when Draper stormed in and reminded Bastien that he'd slept with a prostitute before, and I had two lifetimes I had to consider.

Mad growled when we reached the portal, jerking me back to the present. The few soldiers who stood near the entrance to the next world left us, scattering at one look from the forbidding Untouchable. I almost wished the soldiers hadn't left, though, because now there were good-byes to suffer through. I wasn't sure I had any more tears in me. Reyn hugged Link and Annabelle, and bowed respectfully to Mad. Judah and Draper did the same, and grabbed the first seat up.

I didn't offer to ride up with Judah. I knew that Bastien would have a conniption if I was out of his sight. We'd been parted too often to be cool through even the smallest separations. We were both pretty shaken, especially with the new Vampire twist to our relationship. Instead of feeling weird around each other, we were now one of those couples who were attached at the hip. There were worse things to be, I guess. Still, it was a steep learning curve we were still adjusting to.

Lane wept on Link's shoulder, the emotions of leaving her homeland coming to a head in the emotionally-stunted man's arms. It was better than falling apart in Mad's arms, I guess, but not by much. Link looked like he was actively juggling three lemons in the air, unsure where to hold Lane as she broke down. "There, there?" he guessed, and then started stammering nonsensically when I rolled my eyes at his lame attempt to comfort my mother.

Mad sensed he might be next, so he backed away and positioned Annabelle in front of him, bracing himself from the affection that made him itch.

"Thank you for rescuing my Rosie from those men,"

she blubbered. Her face was wet as she kissed Link's stubbled cheek. "And thank you for rescuing me. If you hadn't come, I don't know what I would've done. I would still be tied there, letting those awful soldiers..." Her sentence cut off as she hiccupped her gratitude on Link's shoulder.

Finally, Link seemed to grow a brain when his eyes connected with mine. I gave him a solemn nod, letting him know that all a man had to do was be kind, and give the woman in his arms a safe place to fall apart until she was ready to put herself back together. Link took a deep breath and banded his arms around my mother, proving that there were good men in the world. "There, there. You're safe now, wee Duchess."

Lane laughed through her tears at the nickname only Link could get away with.

He pulled back to look down at her. "Or are ye my mammy now, too? Bastien's my brother, and he'll soon be your son."

A tender and precious look crossed Lane's features, letting Link know that he'd burrowed into her heart and opened up a whole new facet of love for her to tap into. She leaned up on her toes and pressed a kiss to his forehead. "Thank you, my boy. My sweet son." She paused for the cutie pie blush that crept up the tips of Link's ears. "Come visit us whenever you like." She'd given him instructions on how to reach us in our world, not that we expected he'd ever try to. Link belonged to Faîte, so that's where he would stay. Lane owned a P.O. Box in the town nearest the well, and she'd given the address to Kerdik, Lot, Link and Mad. She promised that as soon as we put down permanent roots, she would leave a card with a burner phone and our address inside the P.O. Box.

Lane pinched Link's cheeks, making him smile in that adorable way you do when your mother embarrasses you in front of your friends. She kissed Annabelle, and exchanged respectful bows with Mad. "Thank you for agreeing to marry my Rosie when she needed you. And thank you for looking out for us."

Mad narrowed his eyes at her. "Aye. Go on, now. I don't need ye hugging me and making a scene."

It was Mad's way of saying goodbye, which Lane respected. She knelt down and hugged Annabelle once more. "You give this hug to your papa, but save it for a time when he looks like he really needs it, okay?"

"Aye, Duchess."

Reyn and Lane caught the swing when it came back down the narrow passageway. I didn't like the unease I felt at being in a different world than Draper, and even worse at the separation from Judah. Reyn took his time situating Lane, who straddled him. Each of them held a pack of clothes and provisions, and a separate bag of jewels. Lane was firm that we would never be homeless again, so each of us had as many of our belongings as possible, plus a backpack of gold and jewels. As we'd still left whole treasure troves for Lot, I didn't begrudge girlfriend whatever she wanted to take with us.

I stood to the side as Bastien said his quiet goodbyes to Link and Mad, hugging them both in that unshakable Brotherhood way that tugged at my deadened heartstrings. The two made a promise that they would come and visit in the next five years, which didn't feel like a solid "I'll see you soon."

I waited for the swing to come down, hoping they'd count my casual wave as an adequate goodbye. I'd been abandoned enough and left too many people to count. I couldn't say goodbye to the Untouchables again. They'd been my... They'd been *mine*. Had I another twenty years living with them, it still wouldn't be enough.

I chanted in my head for the swing to hurry and come back down already as Bastien wrapped up his farewells.

"Rosie, come here," Link demanded, an edge in his tone. I knew he was mad that I had my back to them, ready to bolt.

The swing finally came into sight, and I heaved a gust of relief. "I'll see you guys around," I said without turning to face my goodbyes. When Bastien was still standing with them, I positioned myself on the swing and started pulling myself up. "I'll give you guys some time. See you up there."

32

SCARECROW AND THE TIN MAN

"*R*osie!" Link shouted, clearly hurt that I was ditching out on one last back-and-forth with him.

I didn't want to wound Link, but I knew I couldn't say goodbye to him. I didn't have it in me. I was mentally and emotionally spent, and well past broken. I yanked myself up with the pulley, breathing easier with the distance.

I startled and nearly fell off the swing when I felt something hard tug on my ankle. The hand wrapped around my leg again, and this time I did fall, tumbling the few feet down into Mad's beefy and overlong arms. I squirmed like a fish trying to get back into the safer waters, but he was just as stubborn and far stronger. "Did ye really think ye could run off like tha? Tha I don't deserve so much as a goodbye?"

I twisted in his arms, not making any progress. "I can't

do it, Mad! If I say it, it'll be real, and I can't handle another ounce of reality. Let me go!"

Mad set me down, his expression stern enough to make me stop trying to escape. My chest moved unevenly, and I couldn't meet his eyes. He spoke in his harsh cadence that, over our time together, I'd grown to find comforting. "Tell me goodbye, and tha you'll look after Bastien for us."

My arms banded around my stomach, as if that could keep my guts from spilling out all over the packed dirt. "Goodbye, Mad. I'll make sure Bastien's safe. I'll look after him for you."

Mad's finger went under my chin to keep me from staring at my shoes. "Grand. Now tell me you'll lose a lot of sleep missing us. Not Avalon. Not the others. Link and me. Tell me it'll tear ye up."

I shook my head, unable to get out any more words.

"Tell me," Mad demanded, making himself about as vulnerable as he got. When bossing me wasn't working, he pulled me in for the hug he swore up and down he hated and didn't need. "Tell me," he said, though the plea was softer this time.

I remained stiff in his arms, punching my fist on his shoulder every time I started a fresh sentence. The angst in me welled, choking me and reminding me that I was choosing to leave this man that I loved. I was choosing to break my own heart, and I hated myself for this sin of all sins.

"I'll miss you every day so badly, I won't be able to say

your name for at least a few months. I'll change the subject whenever anyone talks about you two, and lock myself in the bathroom so I can cry without everyone seeing how terrible it is to love someone as much as I love you two, and then having to live without you. I love you so much that I hate you – hate that I have to live without someone who I didn't even know existed a year ago. I hate that I need you, and I love that you let me, and never called me out on it. But I do. I need you, Mad. You were right when you guys said that by marrying Bastien, I'd be marrying all of you. That's what this feels like – leaving a man who I deeply and truly love."

Mad's eyebrows rose. "I didn't mean ye had to say all tha."

I chuckled into his shirt. Then I leaned up on my toes and pecked his lips. "Tell me I didn't ruin your life by dragging you into mine."

He brushed my hair back from my forehead with both hands, and then cupped my face, swallowing my cheeks with his overlarge mitts. "I was ruined long before I met ye. It's only when ye came along tha I had purpose again. Started breathing. T'was a long time since I'd breathed." He growled at the guys to look away, so they didn't gawk at him for being sweet to me. Then he leaned down and kissed me again, drawing out my lower lip. "Ye were a grand wife, Rosie."

I was about to reply when Link scooped me up in his arms and ran back toward the heart of the compound.

"Tha's it! Ye aren't going back to Common. You're staying here with us."

"Link! Put me down, you monkey!"

Link slowed, dropping me to my feet, but he kept my torso pinned to his body in a tight hug. He squeezed me without talking for half a minute, and then finally broke the tense silence with a loud raspberry to the mark on my neck. His lips brushed my ear as he spoke permanence and affection straight into my trembling heart. "Remember whose prize ye are. You're Untouchable, wee Rose. If any of the lads in Common give ye grief, send for me and I'll bend them into pretzels for ye."

I didn't waste any more time, but went straight for the core of it, gripping the nape of Link's neck to keep his cheek pinned to mine. "I want you to smile all the time, have lots of adventures and enjoy as many women who are lucky enough to get you into their beds." Link chuckled, but I wasn't finished. "But when you find the one you want to stay a second night with, don't throw her away. Move Heaven and earth to make it work with her, the way you moved Heaven and earth to give me a better life."

"Aw, ye know I won't be settling down. Tha's the thing about monkeys." He kissed my neck tattoo, and when he pulled back, I felt moisture from his tears on my skin. He buried his face in my neck again, partly to hide his tears, and partly to keep his next confession just between us. "I only had Mad before ye. The Brotherhood is grand, but Bastien was a hermit and the others aren't much better. No one gets our language, our world, the way ye did." He drew in a stuttering breath that made me hold him tighter, alarmed at his sudden bend toward falling apart. "If ye were thinking about staying, then don't go. Not yet, at least. I never got to show ye my homeland. Ye can leave after a few months of a little more time with us. Please, Rosie. We need ye to keep us soft. Without tha, we get old." He clutched me tighter, a quiet panic gripping him in the same way it had me when I thought about leaving him. "I don't want to be old yet!"

It was my turn to hold him together, and I didn't take that responsibility lightly. So rare was it for my Untouchables to admit they needed anything or anyone. After all the downward spirals my life had taken, there in my arms was proof that I was one of the lucky ones. "Hey, it's alright, honey. Link, I'm here. We'll see each other again. And you know how to find us, right? If you need me, come to Common. I'll make sure there's a room for you, Mad and Annabelle, okay?"

"What if I said I need ye now? What then?"

I smiled against his cheek, running my fingers through the small hairs that tickled his neck. "You have me now, silly boy. I love you, Link. You travel with your own portable sunshine. It's me you should be crying for, having to live in Common without your smile."

"Then ye should stay. Come stay in Éireland with me, Mad and Annabelle. We'd treat ye like a queen there." He hugged me and then straightened, lifting my toes off the ground so he could wrap my legs around his waist. I felt weightless and precious in his burly arms. "If there's no one to come home to, lads like me tend not to have a home at all. Don't go."

"I don't belong here," I confessed. "That you love me when there's barely enough pieces of me left to be a whole person? I don't understand it, but I need it. I'll remember that glow in your eyes when I start over up there, and I'll take it with me wherever I go."

Link frowned and looked down at his chest. "Take off my necklace."

"Is it itching you?" I unhooked it and massaged the back of his neck.

"I want ye to wear it. Look in the mirror and remember that Mad and I love ye." He pressed his forehead to mine. "I know it's not as fancy as your rings, but my mammy gave it to me before I joined the army. She said it would keep me safe and remind me of home. I want ye safe, and to know that we're home to each other."

I gasped. "No, Link. I can't. Not a chance. It's too special."

"*You're* too special. Take it."

"But you don't have anything to remind you of me!"

"Aye. I have your smile, the dagger ye gave me from the treasury yesterday, and this." He closed the breath of a gap between us and kissed my lips, ignoring Bastien's hiss of frustration.

Over and over, Link kissed me, reminding me that

there would never be anything between us that could sever our connection – not in Avalon, and not in Common. When his tongue sneaked past my lips, it was a pledge that he wasn't afraid of my sharper teeth, or any parts of me that even I was still frightened of.

I guess that's the thing about warriors. They're not afraid of you, even when there's plenty of evidence that the fight for redemption is doomed.

Link tasted like tears, so I was gentle with him, slowing the pace of the kiss that tugged at my tender insides.

"Does everyone feel free rein to just up and kiss my fiancée whenever they feel like? Look at the ring on her finger, Link. Stop kissing my girlfriend." Bastien pointed at Mad, too. "That goes double for you. Next time either of you gets a girlfriend, I'm kissing her nice and good and in public. There might even be tongue. You've been warned."

Link paid Bastien no mind when he kissed me again, parting our lips a little more so he could sweep his tongue across mine again. "I love ye, wee Rose. Be safe up there, and come for me when it's not safe."

"I will. Same goes for you. If you're scared, come and get me. I'll watch over you."

The corner of Link's mouth lifted in a wry smile. "You'll take care of me?"

"I always do. You're my Lucky Charm." I leaned in and sighed against his cheek, inhaling the scent of his sweat and cologne. "Don't wait five whole years to come visit. Seriously. That's ridiculous." I swallowed hard, my temple pressed to his. "Lie to me, Link. Tell me you'll come over soon. My heart can't take all this breaking."

Link kissed me one more time, and then set me down so he could wipe his eyes. "Aye. Go back to your lad, now. Take care of him and make sure he puts a baby in ye first thing."

I guffawed. "Gross! Don't say it like that. You're such a caveman."

Link shrugged and pointed two fingers to Bastien. "Ye heard me. I want a nephew I can swing in the air by the time I come visit. None of these delicate wee babies I have to be careful with." He blanched. "Hey, Rosie?"

"Yeah, Link?"

There seemed to be a million more goodbyes he wanted to say, but he chose the best one either of us could think of. "'I like it when ye call me Big Poppa.'"

I closed the gap between us again and jumped into his arms, letting my body crash to his so I could feel the treasure of his heartbeat. "See you soon, Big Poppa."

Bastien sat on the plank, all four packs situated over his corded arms. I kissed the top of Annabelle's head, and turned from the three. My limbs were trembling as I threaded my legs around Bastien, clinging to the man I would've stayed in Avalon with, had he asked me. Luckily, Bastien loved me enough not to request I stay somewhere that was bad for us. He blew out a nervous breath at leaving behind the Brotherhood that had seen us both through far too much.

Slowly, the light disappeared as Bastien pulled us up the long, dank shaft. My heart started pounding wildly in my chest at the closed-in feeling I was far too acquainted with, having spent my fair share of time in dark wells.

Bastien understood my creeping anxiety and stopped our upward progression. "Hey, I'm right here. It's you and me now, okay? We're done looking over our shoulders."

My eyes met his in the trickle of light that filtered down from above. "Do you really think that's possible? I can't even picture what that would look like anymore."

"It looks like this." Bastien leaned in and kissed my lips, bracing us on the ropes so we only fell for each other, and not down into the abyss.

Oh, how I loved to fall for Bastien. He nipped at my lips even after the kiss came to a crest. His voice was low and filled with a need that only I could satiate. "That's what I should've done the last time we were in this well. I should've kissed you right then so you would've known how much I want you, how much I loved you from the very beginning."

My arms tightened around his middle. "You loved me all the way back then?"

"Oh, Daisy. I didn't have a chance." He kissed my lips once more. "Are you hungry?"

My neck shrunk guiltily. "I'll be alright. I can last a few more hours."

"Yeah, but this might be our only time alone for a while. I know you don't like to eat in front of the others. Go ahead. Just a little taste." He craned his head to the side, exposing the jugular that sang to me tempting songs of the deepest kind of lust.

"Hello, you'll drop us. It's okay, Bastien."

"Don't you know by now? I've got you." He kept his neck exposed, knowing I was too mortified to ask for what I needed.

My teeth latched onto the flesh just behind his shoulder, puncturing only a little, so I didn't make a mess. Bastien and I both let out sensuous groans of pain and pleasure that fueled carnivorous pelvic thrusts we couldn't control. We probably looked and sounded like we were having sex, but that was the nature of the Vampire and her mate, I guess. Pretty difficult to do discreetly in public. How Bastien managed to keep us from plummeting to the ground, I'll never know.

I pulled away, licking his skin clean over and over until the slight trickle of blood clotted. Bastien was covered in goosebumps, shivering on the seat as he tried to keep still for me. He bit down on his lower lip while I resituated his shirt, holding onto the ropes so we didn't crash.

"We're getting a house," he declared, his voice determined and breathy. "We're getting a house and a bedroom with a bed. We're breaking in that mattress nice and good, and you're going to do that to me again and again until I can't take anymore."

Though he'd assured me he loved our private meals, the whole thing felt like he should be running away from me. The devotion in his caramel eyes only burned more fiercely, tying us more tightly together. He was nearly as addicted to the connection as I was. Bastien seemed to need to give his blood almost as much as I needed to take it. The hunger burned on both our ends, binding us together in ways that made us one of those couples who couldn't be apart.

"You sure you're not freaked out by me yet?"

His eyes were lidded as a shudder ran through him, rocking us both on our precarious perch. "Like I said: house, bedroom, bed, more of that. More of you. Always more."

I licked my lips clean and gave him a break, pulling us upward so we could face the sun, and start our new life in Common together.

33

BRINGING THE FAIRYTALE HOME

"You look nervous," Bastien commented as he tore off the tie I'd picked for him. "This thing is impossible. I'm not wearing it."

"But look at how pretty this blue is! I thought you'd look dashing in it." I slid the silk from his fist and gently looped it around his neck. Pressing a kiss to his pout, I took my time with the knot, making sure it was loose enough so he didn't choke himself while trying to tear the thing off again. A few people shot us curious looks, being so dressed up at the Justice of the Peace on a Tuesday. The courtroom was unromantic, but us being there filled the halls with a brush of beauty and whimsy. We brought the fairytale with us wherever we went, and never apologized for it. "See? I was right. Handsome."

"I said I wanted to marry you, not be trussed up like a turkey."

"Think of it this way," I said, leaning up on my toes so I could whisper in his ear. "If you wear the tie and the jacket for the ceremony, I promise to strip every scrap of clothing off of you the fun way tonight. What do you think about that, Mr. Avalon?" Bastien and Reyn had agreed to take our last names, which was good, since they didn't have any for us to take.

Bastien gazed down at my white satin strapless gown. Well, I called it a gown, but the saleswoman informed me that it was a cocktail dress. Whatever. I was a bride, so this would be a gown. Bastien's eyes were hungry for me, staring at my curves like a teenager. I loved that I brought out the teenager in Bastien. He was such an old man otherwise. "I can deal with the tie, I guess."

When Lane came out of the bathroom, her eyes darted around nervously for Reyn. "I feel like I should go change."

I tugged on Lane's arm, but her eyes were wide with fear. I squeezed Bastien's hand. "Give us a couple of minutes, alright? We'll meet you guys in there."

"Okay. Take your time. You look beautiful, Mom." Bastien had taken to claiming Lane as his mom, partly to remind me that I had a parent who wanted me, and would cross worlds just to be near me.

"Thank you, Son." Lane all but jerked me into the bathroom, waiting until the door shut behind us to motion to her dress. "Would you look at this nonsense?"

My eyes searched for a stain, but the white was unmarked. "What? I don't see anything. It's perfect. Other than the crazy face you're making, you're a ten in a world of sixes if I ever saw one."

Self-loathing painted her features as she banded her arms across her breasts, looking like she might vomit. "A woman who's been passed around as much as me doesn't have a right to wear white on her wedding day. I feel... I'm dirty now. I don't belong in something this pure."

My eyebrows furrowed as I threw myself on her in a tight hug, covering her shame-filled parts with my body to shield her from her own condemnation. "I love you," I said like a promise. "You are not dirty, and you're not passed around. You're a bride on her wedding day. You should wear whatever color you want, and white was the winner. Would you tell me not to wear white if that had happened to me?"

"Of course not. It's not the same, though. This feels..." She dug her nails into me, so we could endure her pain together. "Why does he still want me?"

I pulled back, staring into the eyes that had only ever held love and goodness for me. "Because you're you. Those soldiers didn't take that away. Know who you are, Lane. Reyn sees you clearly. He gets what a catch you are." I kissed her forehead. "*I* know who you are. The girl I love should wear the prettiest dress from the best store in town, which is what this is."

Lane sucked in the tears before they could fall and nodded, taking a steadying breath. "You're right. I know who I am." She glanced in the mirror, trying to summon up the confidence she'd once had on tap. "I wanted to wear a wedding dress, so that's what I'm going to do." She raised her chin in defiance of the white form-fitting gown that was almost the exact same as mine, except there was a lace layer over hers that stretched two inches above her cleavage, and hung two inches below the knee-length hemline. The long lace sleeves and the perfect low-set bun made her look elegant, fresh off a forties Hollywood movie set. Lane was a sight to be reckoned with, which was pretty much no different than every other day of her life. She squared her shoulders with a cool look of manufactured confidence, turned to me and said, "They're not going to know what hit them."

"That's my girl. Let's do this."

With our hands clasped, we glided into the hallway of the courthouse like twin brides looking for trouble. Bastien moved with us, walking in step with me as we always did these days. So much of our time together had been spent out of step, but after I turned Vampire, something seemed to click in us both. We were done being stupid. We were done messing up a good thing.

Reyn, Draper and Judah stood, straightening their ties and smoothing out their suit jackets when we rounded the corner. The look on Reyn's face took my breath away – so enraptured with Lane was every fiber of his being. He looked dapper in his suit, making me smirk with affection that I was getting a new dad who was super way kind and totally wonderful.

The ceremony was quick, the kisses were sweet, and the certificates were signed and promptly filed. I couldn't believe how easy our world made it for us to finally be together after being pulled apart for so long.

When our car rolled into the ten-acre plot of land we'd traded a few jewels to secure, our giddy grins quickly soured, and then died as confusion settled in. Gasps rippled around the interior of the SUV when we saw that the formerly grass-covered grounds were now utterly blooming with thousands of yellow roses. I mean, thousands. Lane's jaw was practically on the floor. "What did that son of a gun do this time?"

I let out a swear, covering my mouth as Bastien's fist tightened. "We're married now. I thought he was supposed to be in Avalon. Rosie, why is Kerdik sniffing around our place?"

"I honestly don't know, Bastien. I had no idea. Lane?"

"No clue, baby. I don't see him, though. Maybe he just stopped by to..." She shook her head. "I've got nothing."

Reyn, Bastien and Draper wore grim expressions as they stepped out of the black vehicle. Judah stayed with us in the car, locking the doors as if that could stop Kerdik. "'Your boyfriend's back, and you're gonna be in trouble,'" he sang just to get a rise out of me.

"Shut up. What's that? Bastien's carrying something."

Judah unlocked the doors and let us out when Bastien ruled that Kerdik wasn't here (as if I should be afraid of Kerdik. I mean, sheesh). He shoved a box at me with a closed expression that told me this was not the time for Kerdik – as if I didn't already know that. "This came for you and Lane. Whatever it is, the answer's no."

"I know. Jeez. I didn't do this, Bastien."

"The day we get married shouldn't be the day your boyfriend shows up with gifts and flowers."

"I didn't..." I rolled my eyes and huffed. "Do you want me to open it?"

"No, *I* will. I'm your *Guardien*, and this is a package from a dangerous immortal." He took the box back and ripped off the top as if he wished it was Kerdik's face he could destroy. Then Bastien's eyebrows furrowed in confusion.

"Well?"

He shrugged and handed Lane the white box.

Lane pulled out a pouch of herbs that looked like the fancy kind of tea only serious hipster tea drinkers invested in. There was a note attached to it addressed to her that she read aloud to the group.

"'DEAR MOTHER,

Drink this tea on your honeymoon if your wish is to carry Reyn's child.'" Lane gasped, her pace picking up as she read the rest in a rush. "'You're the kind of woman who should have as many children as you want. On the day your daughter leaves you to marry the man of her choice, the only gift that seems fitting is to give you a child to fill the hole that losing someone like Rosie marks a person with. On your child's first birthday, I will come to visit with a birth blessing for your baby.'"

Tears fell hard and fast from Lane's cheeks, dotting the white paper and making Kerdik's perfect calligraphy bleed.

Reyn's hands were shaking when he took the note to read it over, verifying that the thing he'd made his peace with not having was actually within his grasp. "Lane, tell me we can make a baby this very night." He kissed her in front of all of us, making everyone but me tear up. I'd long since suppressed my urges to cry, instead digging my nails into my arm to release a little of the building emotion.

Lane looked from the note to Reyn with tears sparkling on her lashes. "You want to have a baby with me?"

"Only with you. Come inside. We've got plenty of time before we have to be to the airport. I'll start some water brewing." Reyn all but dragged the giddy Lane into their white farmhouse, not bothering to tell the rest of us to scram. We got the hint well enough.

Draper and Judah looked away with mixed emotions on their faces. They were happy Lane would be a mother again, but didn't feel so hot knowing their adopted mommy was about five minutes away from knocking boots in the house we all stood awkwardly outside.

I lifted out an envelope, handing it to Judah out of habit. My ring sparkled in the sunlight. The two sets of three aquamarines in a triangle cluster from my wedding band encased both sides of the square-shaped diamond on my engagement ring. It was the exact opposite of the configuration on my right hand from Kerdik, and looked too beautiful for someone like me to wear without people assuming it was costume jewelry.

Judah shot Bastien an apologetic look before he began reading.

"'DEAR ROSIE,

The vase of roses inside are to keep with you until you bring them home to me when you return to Avalon someday. They possess a warding charm, so that anyone seeking you out with ill intent will have a more difficult time locating you. Not impossible, but the delay should give Bastien enough time to figure out an intruder is coming.

Be kind to your husband. I fear I've made him suffer much.

Truly Yours,
Kerdik'"

BASTIEN'S TEETH GROUND TOGETHER. "I SWEAR, IF HE DIDN'T just help keep you safer, then I'd be pissed he snuck onto our property to leave you gifts. It's like he's trying to pee all over you to mark his territory." Then Bastien raised his voice. "*My* home, you hear? This is *my* home, and Rosie is *my* wife!"

It was Judah's laugh that broke the tension as he handed me the note. "Kerdik cracks me up. I mean, what a dick move! You get married, and bam! Dude sends you magical flowers and re-landscapes the whole property to remind you he's still around." He clapped in Kerdik's honor. "Ballsy, that's for sure." Judah looped his arm around my shoulders and led me away so Draper could talk Bastien down.

I grimaced, pinching the bridge of my nose as we walked a few steps away from Bastien's ranting. "Yikes. I didn't think Kerdik would ever come to Common."

"He's in love with you, Ro. Not sure why you're always underestimating how far people will go to keep you around."

"Oh, you."

He stopped walking and turned me to him, holding my shoulders so he had my full attention. "I feel like we need to have the talk. You know, *the* talk."

I groaned, rolling my eyes. "Hello, I'm twenty-three. And you tutored me through sex ed. Don't think I don't remember your totally gross hand puppets."

Judah sniggered. "I forgot about those. I'm brilliant. Just remember, he's supposed to stick it in your ear. That's how I never got Jill pregnant. But make sure he wears protection, otherwise you won't be able to hear for a week."

I belted out a laugh at his stupid joke. "Will do." Then it began to dawn on me that this was actually happening. I was excited, but a little bit nervous at crossing this giant milestone. "It's probably dorky of me to be glad my best friend is a telephone tin can call away, just in case." Yes, we'd installed a telephone tin can system that went from my bedroom to Judah's, because we're awesome, and we can. He was staying in the smaller house that Draper lived in on our property until Judah decided what he wanted to do with his life.

"I'm always a phone call away, Ro. Never forget that." Judah slapped my palm with the secret handshake we'd made up back in the fifth grade, when we both realized we were the coolest people in our class. Then he chucked my shoulder with a wicked grin. "Time to cowboy up, Hot Mama."

"Thanks, Pimp Daddy."

Once Bastien had calmed down, he led me to our farmhouse, which was further back on our shared property. Judah and Draper were granted their very own bachelor pad that rested between my house and Lane's. I loved the land we lived on, even more when it was filled with yellow roses. Bastien scowled at the flowers as if they were offensive, which I guess they kind of were. "When I die, I'm haunting Kerdik for the rest of eternity. That'll be my mission in the afterlife. He's in for some serious ghostly hijinks."

"I married you, you know. We're technically on our honeymoon."

Bastien's shoulders relaxed as he shut the door behind

us. The blue accents on the cream walls greeted us like a calming hug. I couldn't get enough of it all. It was our very own haven nestled next to the woods. Our ritual was to go for hikes through the thick trees every night before we went to bed.

Bastien didn't waste a moment, lest Kerdik snatch away the night we'd been waiting so very long to indulge in. My husband scooped me up in his arms and charged up the stairs to our bedroom. I adored the cheery yellow walls that greeted us, and the king-sized bed that seemed to give us a sexy come hither. Even though we had the whole house to ourselves, I gasped at the scandal when Bastien didn't shut our bedroom door as he dumped me on the mattress, peeling off his suit jacket and tie.

I frowned at him, propping myself up on my elbows. "Hey, that was my job. I wanted to take your suit and tie off for you. At least let me do your pants."

"I can't wait, Daisy. I need this dress off of you. I told you, no clothes for a week, starting now."

"Worst game of chicken ever, Ro!" Judah called through his tin can. "I'm disconnecting the line, and we'll reinstall it from your guest room. Happy humping, dudes."

I covered my mouth and let out a nervous laugh in time with Bastien's raised eyebrows. He went over to the window and pushed the can out onto the grass two floors below. The moment was sufficiently derailed, but I knew our love never would be. I sat up on my knees and cupped Bastien's face in my hands, wanting a closer look at the man I loved. Then I kissed my husband, drawing a contented sigh from both of our lips. "Tell me it'll always be like this," I whispered, hanging onto his shoulders.

Bastien leaned down and whispered in my ear, "It'll always be like this because we'll always have each other," he vowed. Then he kissed me once more before he sealed our love with a firm, "I've got you."

Love the book?
Leave a review.

34

COMMON GIRL

Here's a free preview of *Common Girl*, Book 8 in the *Faîte Falling* series, which introduces Celtic folklore.

"My name is Rosie, and I'm an alcoholic," I said, holding onto the podium with white knuckles. A few strands of brown hair fell loose from the messy bun atop my head, but I couldn't let go of the podium to brush them from my face. I waited for the obligatory, "Hi, Rosie," before I continued. "It's been three days since my last drink."

I'd said the same thing for the last six months with literally no change in my status. At every single one of the weekly AA meetings, it was never more than three days since my last hit of blood from Bastien. Sometimes it was that morning I'd broken my fast and meandered glumly into the bedroom to ask for a little snack.

Bastien never minded. In fact, he looked forward to my meals. He loved the fact that I was the *Attelage* kind of Vampire, which meant I could only feed from him. Usually we got so worked up during my meals that we made love right after I drank. He was never reticent to give me as much blood as I wanted, and loved every second of it. He relished being the only one who could sustain me, and drive me as crazy with lust as we did. We'd developed a sort of unquenchable hunger for each other, not wanting to be apart for more than an hour or so. We'd spent too much time trying (and failing) to get together; we didn't waste the gift we'd been granted.

The thing about it was that I didn't want to need blood. It had been a total accident that I'd been infected with Éireland's lost magic. I hadn't even been in Éireland, but was at my mother's castle in Avalon when it all went down, and the lost magic was released back into Faîte. Now I was part Vampire, and part some second benign thing that hadn't shown any symptoms. Bastien's guess was that the second black snake-like strand of magic that had flowed into me after I'd killed my mother and accidentally set all the lost magic loose, was just more Vampire mojo. He reasoned this as the guess why I couldn't go more than three days without gnawing on my own fingers for a hit of my husband's blood. I wanted to be a normal wife. I wanted my stinking 30-day chip.

A middle-aged woman named Marianne had hers now. It was her first one, and she was showing it to everyone like the coveted prize it was. I was proud of her, but part of me wished I could have that kind of discipline.

Bastien was quiet through the meetings we attended every week, but this time as we helped stack up the chairs he paused to kiss my cheek. I loved the way his perpetual five o'clock shadow felt when it brushed against my smooth skin. "I think we should skip next week's meeting," he suggested. "I see how much it tears you up not to have a chip like Marianne's."

I conjured up a smile that told the world I was totally in control, but Bastien saw right through it. "One day I'll get mine."

"This isn't the same thing, and you know it. You can't live without... ketchup." It was our super-secret code word for blood. I know. We're total ninjas. "Living without alcohol is a fine thing for anyone's body. You can't survive without ketchup."

"We've been married for a year and a half now. I've been drinking ketchup for way too long. You'd think I'd get better at this. I mean, you got your one-year bronze chip months ago." My knuckles tightened on the folding chair before I stacked it with the others. "Why can't I get better at this?"

"Me being sober isn't the same thing as what you're trying to do. You're too hard on yourself. It's those nightmares that are making you so down today. You need a solid night's sleep."

"If only. Too many nights of the same creepy dream, and it still makes no sense to me." Every night when I finally fell asleep, a voice came into my mind. He never had a face or a body, just a voice that was low and deep. It was like the best kind of radio DJ, but with an Irish brogue and a penchant for skeeving me out. At first, I hadn't been able to understand him. Now, after months and months of the same nonsensical dream that always left me feeling disturbed and unsettled, through the random syllables I could make out a low command of "Come."

Nothing scary about that, right?

Bastien got me. He didn't freak out or demand we go back to Avalon to see if a healer could find us some answers, but held me patiently when I woke him with my tossing and turning. We made love half-asleep last night, and most nights that I woke him mid-slumber.

"Come here." Bastien pulled me into his embrace, kissing the square-shaped diamond he'd put on my finger. The three aquamarines on each side sparkled up at us, shining as brilliantly as they did the day we'd gotten married at the Justice of the Peace in a quiet joint affair with Lane and Reyn.

Bastien was more relaxed in my world. He smiled easier and laughed often. When he started to hum and turn us in a slow dance only we were invited to, I fell in love with him all over again. He had the smile that could transform the dismal meeting room with drab walls and uncomfortable chairs into a ballroom with merely a slight curve of his perfect lips. He hadn't been the type to dance to woo a woman, but he learned to waltz for me. Bastien had learned so many things, living in my world. We were inseparable and insatiable, and unapologetic on both those points.

"You look hungry. Let's get you home," he suggested, corralling me past the coffee and stale donuts toward the door. "These clothes look like you've been wearing them for too long."

I guffawed. "Hello, it's only one o'clock."

"I need you," he confessed, tucking me into his side as we waved goodbye to the facilitator. "That little red number of yours that we broke in last night? I think it needs a repeat."

I unlocked our car and slid into the driver's seat. "Well, it's not going to get a replay. You ripped it clear down the middle, if you recall. Such a greedy boy."

Bastien adjusted his jeans as he buckled. "You can't scold me like that. You know it makes me crazy. I'm two minutes away from throwing you down in the backseat."

"You know we can't do that; you're too loud."

"Me? I'm not the one the animals were worried about. That was all you."

I blushed at the reminder of the forty some-odd woodland creatures who pelted our farmhouse with pinecones, pebbles and sticks because I screamed so loud in the throes that they thought Bastien was attacking me. Part of my birth blessing was that I could communicate with animals and hear other unknown languages. Using my magic tired me out, which was how I got to sleep every night, since Avalon citizens usually didn't have the need for sleep.

Bastien was my *Guardien*, which meant he used loads of magic to ward our property against intruders and keep me safe. I loved sleeping next to my husband. Our simple life might seem boring to some, but we'd earned a few decades of nothing harrowing tearing us apart. People underestimate boring. Lately, it's been my codename for bliss.

Bastien's hand found its way to my thigh, which was how we always drove. He still didn't have his license, since he was a menace on the road even after all the tutorials Lane and I had given our guys. "Are we babysitting Lucas tonight?" he asked idly, staring out the window.

"Nope. Tonight's bowling. Wednesday night is bowling, Thursday is babysitting our nephew. You think he's learned a new word yet?"

"No," Bastien replied, repeating Lucas' only word. Lane and Reyn got pregnant on their honeymoon. Perhaps before they'd even left on the plane for Barbados. Lucas had that gorgeous mixed-race light brown skin, chubby cheeks, Lane's bright smile, and Reyn's long, curly eyelashes. In short, we didn't have a prayer. Whatever Lucas asked for, we gave him.

Bastien was a mixture of protective and indulgent with Lucas. Did me in every time. "We should really be stricter with him. Last time I fed him he only ate a few bites of dinner, and had like, three suckers."

I shrugged. "It's our rite as his favorite aunt and uncle. Disciplining's for the parents. The spoiling's for us to do."

Bastien squeezed my thigh, and I could almost guess the question that flowed out from his luscious lips before it came. "You sure you want to wait three years before we have a baby?"

"I'm sure. I like our life as it is. And if you try and hide my birth control again, you'll only be shooting yourself in the foot. We've never gone a whole two days without sex, but you'll be staring down the barrel of a drought if you do that again. I'm this close to getting the shot just to nip that in the bud."

"Okay, okay. Just so you know my vote, I'd get you nice and pregnant right now. Say the word, and we can pull over and make us a baby."

I shot him a squinty eye. "Three years. I still don't have my degree yet."

"That reminds me, do we need to cut bowling short so you can study with Judah over Skype tonight? You've got those two finals next week."

"Nah. Bowling is sacred. I wouldn't dream of calling that off. I'm mostly prepared." Man, I hoped that was true. I'd been studying for these finals for weeks, staying after class with my professors and studying all the live-long day. I listened to recordings of the lectures over and over again until I felt confident enough to go out at night without feeling like failing grades were going to come toppling down on my head. Oh, the joys of being dyslexic.

"You think your freaky dreams will go away once the stress of finals is over?"

I shrugged. "Couldn't hurt. I was thinking we should go camping or something in the mountains to celebrate my last semester being over – pass or fail."

"You'll pass. You'll do great. And I'd love to go camping again."

"Want to take Lucas, and give Reyn and Lane some time together?"

"I really, really don't. Love the little guy, but I've got big plans for you. Big celebrating plans that involve things children can't be around for."

My lips drew to the side as if in thought. "Hmm. Things children can't be around for. Are we going to do our taxes? No, tax season is over. Are we going to talk politics?"

Bastien leaned over and whispered in detail several un-utterable things he'd been wanting to try. He tugged my earlobe between his teeth, making me shiver as I pulled onto the main road.

A shudder rippled through my body in anticipation of all he was promising. "Well, I guess Lucas can stay home if we're going to be giving *that* a try."

Start Book 8 in the *Faîte Falling* series,
and read *Common Girl* today!

ABOUT THE AUTHOR

USA Today bestselling author Mary E. Twomey lives in Michigan with her three adorable children. She enjoys reading, writing, vegetarian cooking, and telling her children fantastic stories about wombats.

While she loves writing fantasy, dystopian, and paranormal tales for her readers, Mary also writes romance under the name Tuesday Embers, and cozy mysteries under the name Molly Maple.

Visit her online at www.maryetwomey.com, and sign up for her newsletter, so you never miss a new release.

www.ingramcontent.com/pod-product-compliance
Lightning Source LLC
Chambersburg PA
CBHW010317100726
47906CB00006B/1031